Dating Breena

BECKI LEE

LITERARY ESCAPES PRESS

Contents

For women everywhere who lift each other up

Want a FREE book?

Grab the Prequel to the Nashville Hearts series HERE! (https://beckileeauthor.com/rescuing -hope/)

Chapter 1

BREENA

B REENA ROLLED HER STIFF shoulders, pushed her hair out of her face, and read the email for the tenth time, debating, yet again, whether she should push send.

Dear Mr. Simmonds,

My name is Breena Renee O'Malley; I'm your daughter.

My mother, Maeve O'Malley, never mentioned your name, and it's taken years for an investigator to track you down.

I've debated whether I should even reach out, but one question keeps popping up for me.

Why?

Why did you choose to not be part of my life? To not have anything to do with me for thirty-plus years?

Respectfully,

Breena

She held her breath and pushed send, unsure what, if anything, would happen next. She closed her laptop and looked at the two large yellow envelopes on the desk next to it. She'd picked them up earlier from her lawyer, Mr. Pillingham, and decided it was time for some answers.

One was labeled Maeve Erin O'Malley, for the mother who abandoned her when she was nine years old. She hadn't yet been brave enough to open that envelope. But the other was labeled Peter Simmonds—her father, a man who'd *never* been in her life. Had never wanted her.

She stared sightlessly out her bedroom window overlooking the downtown Nashville skyline. Neon lights shining twenty-five stories below her broke up the darkness and made snow flurries appear colorful.

The penthouse she lived in with her best friend, Grace, had belonged to Grace's mother, Marilyn. When Marilyn passed away the previous year, it had come as a shock to both Grace and Breena that the woman who'd raised them both had been a multimillionaire and had left a generous inheritance for each of them.

Breena yawned and decided any further action regarding her birth parents could wait until morning. After setting the envelopes on her dresser, she turned off her light and settled underneath a soft, white down comforter. Just as she was starting to fall asleep, her cell phone rang.

"Hello?" She answered with another yawn. She knew if someone were calling at—she glanced at her clock—two in the morning, it must be important.

"Bree, it's Jilly. I'm sorry to wake you, but are you up for a guest tonight?" Jillian, a Nashville police officer, was one of her best friends and Grace's soon-to-be sister-in-law.

"No problem. How far out are you?" Breena sat up, alert, all thought of her parents driven from her head.

"About fifteen minutes."

Breena could hear the background noise of traffic and sirens. "Okay, I'll be ready for you."

She hopped out of bed and pushed aside the prospect of sleep as she scrambled into a set of scrubs. She pulled her long, wavy, dark red hair into a scrunchy, then went into her closet and pushed a small button in the back-right corner of the floor. The back wall silently slid open to expose a hidden apartment. Before disappearing through the opening, she shot off a text to Grace, asleep at the other end of the penthouse.

BREENA: We have a guest.

The layout of the secret apartment was similar to the one she lived in, except two of the three bedrooms had been converted to other purposes. One was an exam room, akin to the setup in a hospital, but homier and unquestionably more comfortable. The second room was designed to be a gym or physical therapy room.

Marilyn, Grace's mother, had set up this secret apartment to provide a safe temporary shelter for abused women. She never knew who would be coming through or what they might need. And now Grace and Breena were doing their best to continue her mission by helping women in this apartment until Grace's long-term shelter, Hope's House, was completed.

Quickly and efficiently, Breena made a pot of coffee, knowing she would not be the only one who would need it tonight...well, this morning. She checked the exam room and made sure everything was in order.

Just as she finished her first cup of coffee, the doors to the elevator slid open, and Jillian and Brian, the building's burly doorman, walked in. Brian was carrying a woman with long honey-blonde hair matted around her face, which was bloody and already turning dark colors.

"Go to the exam room. It's all ready." Breena washed her hands, then followed them into the room.

Brian gently placed the woman on the bed, and Breena got to work doing what she knew best—how to help others and be the nurse she was trained to be.

"Has anyone taken pictures yet?" she asked, gathering supplies.

"No, we weren't sure if we should," Jillian said.

Confused, Breena looked at her friend. "Why wouldn't we want pictures?"

Jillian nodded her head toward the bed. Breena looked at the woman and inhaled sharply, understanding dawning. The woman on her exam bed was none other than Laci Love.

The Laci Love.

The biggest singing sensation to come out of Nashville in years.

She was the sweetheart of country music.

Breena looked at the woman again and nodded in understanding. "We still need the pictures. We just need to be incredibly careful to make sure the press doesn't see them. But if she wants to press charges, she'll need evidence. I got this. Coffee's fresh, help yourselves."

Brian and Jillian left the exam room, and Breena got to work. Someone had used this beautiful woman as a punching bag, and her bloody face was starting to swell. Breena grabbed her phone and clipboard and began documenting her newest guest.

"I'm Breena," she said softly when Laci groaned. "I'm going to clean you up and help you into something more comfortable."

Laci nodded, understanding. "Wait...why are you taking pictures? No pictures." Her words were soft and slightly slurred.

"I don't know who did this to you, but if you ever want to press charges, you'll need these pictures for evidence. I won't let them out of my possession, but this is our only opportunity to get them."

Laci sighed and nodded again, a tear running down her bruised cheek.

"I'm sorry if this hurts, but I need to get you out of these clothes." Slowly, gently, and methodically, Breena cut the torn and bloody outfit off her guest, cleaned her up, then helped her into a soft gown.

By the time she'd finished, she'd noted Laci had a black eye, a shallow laceration along her hairline, bruises on her face and arms, and a couple of bruised ribs. "I'm going to give you something for the pain to help you sleep a bit easier."

"I don't want any drugs."

"This is over the counter. Not addictive, not too strong. Things are going to start hurting, and I'd like you to be as comfortable as possible."

Laci nodded, swallowed the pills, and lay back on the soft bed. "Who are you?"

"I'm Breena."

"But why are you helping me? Where am I?" She looked around the room. It was pale pink with white sheers on the window. There was an antique dresser full of supplies against one wall and a comfy dark-gray recliner next to the bed. "Obviously, this isn't a hospital."

Breena looked around the room as well and smiled. "You're right, this isn't a hospital. You're in my home, and you're safe. I'm not sure what happened to you, but when women are brought to me, it's because they need a place to hide from someone...or in your case, I'd guess *everyone*. This apartment has a history of helping women in need that I'll tell you about later, when you're not so groggy and not in pain." She smiled at Laci, whose eyes were struggling to stay open. "Go ahead and sleep. I'll be here when you wake up."

Breena paused a few minutes to make sure Laci was comfortable and asleep, then went to the living room, where Brian and Jillian sat at the counter, waiting for her, each with a cup of coffee.

"Laci Love?" She looked at Jillian. "What the heck is going on?"

"We responded to a 911 call. She didn't want to go to the hospital but did want to be hidden, so here made the most sense."

Breena nodded toward the exam room. "But who would do this to her?"

"I'm guessing her boyfriend. Looked like he wasn't happy about something tonight. He'd disappeared by the time we got there." Jillian pulled out her phone. "I got pictures of the scene and asked for discretion from the officers processing it. But it's going to be out when the world wakes up."

"Did anyone see you bring her here?" Brian asked.

"No." Jillian shook her head. "As far as the press can tell, an ambulance took her to the hospital. We were able to get her out unseen."

"She's safe here," Breena said. "Hopefully, we can keep it that way. I'll talk to Grace in the morning." She looked at her watch and shook her head. "Well, later this morning. I've got this for now. Go get some sleep, you two."

As they headed out, Breena made another pot of coffee; she wouldn't be getting any sleep. Then she cooked some oatmeal and put some frozen fruit on top before sitting in the comfortable lounge chair next to Laci's bed, going over her notes while her guest slept.

"Hey."

Breena startled at the soft voice and looked up to see Grace standing in the doorway. She checked her watch, eight o'clock, then took a peek at her guest and determined she was still sleeping before heading out to the dining room. She noticed the breakfast tray Grace had brought with her, grateful for her thoughtfulness.

"A new guest, huh?" Grace eyed the room Breena had just come from.

"Yep, and this one has the potential to cause issues."

She saw confusion on Grace's face. Each guest came with their own problems, but this one had the potential to blow their secrecy out of the water.

"Laci Love," she said simply and watched Grace's eyes grow wide.

"Really? Is she okay?" Grace looked back at the exam room, concern on her face.

"She will be. Got a good bang-up, but she'll heal. Physically." Breena gestured to the coffee pot. "Want some?"

Grace nodded, pushing her dark blonde hair off her face and stretching her long, lean body before sitting on one of the stools at the kitchen counter.

"You look beat. What time did you get the call?"

"Thanks. You know how to make a girl feel special." Breena chuckled softly and set a cup of coffee in front of her friend. "Jilly called at two."

"Yikes. I can hang here if you'd like to take a shower and get a nap."

A groan from the exam room brought Breena back in. Laci was waking up, and it sounded like the medicine had worn off enough for her to be uncomfortable.

"Good morning," Breena greeted her guest, doing a quick visual exam. "Where's it hurting?"

"Oh, everywhere." Laci grimaced as she struggled to sit up.

"Hang on, I'll sit your bed up." Breena put a gentle but firm hand on Laci's shoulder to keep her from moving and worked the controls to slowly lift the bed. "You think you can eat?"

Laci closed her eyes. "Yeah. That would be good, I think. Thank you."

Grace came in with a tray loaded with buttered toast, scrambled eggs, a banana, a cup of coffee, and some water. "I wasn't sure what would sound good, but this all seemed like it would be easy to eat."

Laci looked wide-eyed at Breena, fear in her eyes.

"This is Grace Parson. She's my best friend, the owner of this apartment, and my partner in helping the women who come through here. She's safe."

Grace set the tray on a rolling table and adjusted it across the bed.

"Thanks, Grace. This is perfect." Breena smiled at her friend before turning to Laci. "Think you can get any of this down?"

Laci nodded as she took a bite of the toast. She then made quick work of the food, looking a little sheepish. "Guess I was hungry."

Breena chuckled. "That's good though. Now I can give you more medicine to help with the pain."

Laci frowned and shook her head. "I don't like taking drugs. I'd prefer not to."

"You've got some bruised ribs, and they've got to be painful. You don't *have* to take the medicine, but it will certainly help you rest more comfortably. How about just today, then tomorrow we won't do meds? I need to wrap your ribs today, and it is not going to feel good. You might appreciate the pain relief."

Laci shook her head. "No, I'd rather not. And thank you for letting me stay here. I'm guessing the news is already out, so I'll need another spot to hide soon."

"You're safe, Laci." Breena sat in the chair next to the bed and looked Laci in the eye. "No one knows you're here. And they won't. This is a *safe* house, and you are welcome here for as long as you need."

"No one knows I'm here? How is that possible?" Laci looked at her in disbelief. "I know there were reporters at my house last night. Someone had to have followed the police officer who brought me here."

"The reporters followed an ambulance to the hospital. Jillian, the police officer who helped you, was then able to bring you here unnoticed. Like I said, you're safe here." Breena smiled as she stood up to clear away the dishes. "Now let's get you bandaged up so you're a little more comfortable. I'd love for you to rest a bit more."

Breena carefully bandaged Laci's ribs, then lowered the bed back down. Laci was out before she left the room.

"Mind if I take you up on that nap and shower now?" she asked Grace.

"No problem. I got this. I brought a book, and I'll just hang out in there while she rests. I texted Carl to tell him I was spending time with you and our guest this morning, so I'm available as long as you need me." She grinned at her friend. "Honestly, I'm happy to be away from the construction zone up at Hope's House."

"I won't be too long." Grateful, Breena hugged her friend and made her way back through the hidden panel to the main apartment to take a shower and change.

In her own bathroom, Breena surveyed her face in the mirror. Her light Irish skin—Grace always called it peaches-and-cream—was even paler than usual, and her green eyes had purple bruising under them from lack of sleep. She pulled the scrunchy out of her hair and let it tumble down. Growing up, she'd hated her curly red hair, but now it was just part of who she was.

She looked down at her body. She'd always been envious of Grace's tall, slim build. Breena was shorter and curvier. She was getting a little curvier than she wanted. Time to get out and start running again. *Ugh*.

A shower and a two-hour power nap would help. She *knew* how to do naps. After being a nurse for the past ten years, naps were part of her normal routine. She could sleep anywhere. And she'd honed her internal alarm clock so she could wake her up when she needed to. She blasted the hot water and stepped into the shower. The beating water massaged her tired body, loosening her muscles. After her shower, she crawled into bed and immediately fell asleep.

Two hours later, almost to the minute, Breena woke up, ready to tackle the day. She pulled on a pair of black leggings and an emerald-green sweater that fell to midthigh. Before heading next door again, she pulled out the crockpot and assembled ingredients for vegetable soup.

As she walked through the sliding panel in her bedroom closet to the secret apartment, she saw Grace making grilled ham-and-cheese sandwiches.

"Is she awake?" Breena asked, sniffing appreciatively.

"Just woke up and asked about some lunch, so I thought I'd get some sandwiches going. How was the nap?"

"Just what I needed. I feel much better now. Thanks for hanging out so I could nap."

Breena wandered into the exam room to check on their guest. She smiled to see the bed already up and Laci reading a book Grace had brought with her.

"Hey there. How're you feeling?" She walked to the bed and started checking over Laci.

"I feel like I got hit by a truck." Laci grimaced.

"Well, you certainly got hit by something...or some*one*. Let me check your wrapping, then we can try getting up to eat in the dining room."

She knew they'd talk about what happened eventually but didn't want Laci to feel like she had to share before she was ready. Gently helping her out of the gown, she grabbed the supplies and rewrapped her ribs. Laci winced, and Breena was impressed she didn't cry out.

"I have some soft, comfortable clothes we can get you into, then we can see how you feel about walking."

After helping Laci out of the hospital gown and into a pair of sweatpants and a soft button-front, long-sleeved top, Breena helped her off the bed and out to the dining room. The smell of grilled sandwiches permeated the air, and both women's stomachs grumbled in appreciation. They looked at each other and grinned.

With Laci settled at the table, Breena grabbed the plates and silverware as Grace gathered the food. Lunch was quiet as the women ate their sandwiches with some fruit. Breena kept an eye on what Laci ate and was pleased to note she had a good appetite.

"Based on what I see out the window, we're in downtown Nashville. But where exactly are we?" Laci asked between bites.

"We're at The Athenian." Grace grinned at Laci's surprised expression. "Yeah, we were surprised to find this here too. My mother set this apartment up several years ago when she lived here."

Breena jumped into the conversation. "We were flabbergasted when Brian, the doorman who helped you up here, showed us this space. We moved here about three and a half months ago and have just recently been able to restart this mission."

Laci nodded. "Well, I appreciate you letting me stay."

"I want to make sure you're comfortable here, so is there anything I can bring you? Food, clothes, anything?" Grace asked. "I'm running around for a bachelor auction tonight, so I'm happy to pick up whatever you need. I can't go to your house, but I can buy anything we don't already have."

"You're doing the bachelor auction?" Laci looked at her, surprised. "I think my manager, Gabe, is in the auction."

"You mean Gabriel van Neugh? Yep, he's in it." Grace laughed. "He was very wary when Carl and I first approached him about participating."

They talked for a few minutes about face cleansers, lotions, and what size clothes Laci needed before Grace headed out with a promise to be back in a few hours. "If you think of anything else you need or want, just shoot me a text."

"Oh no! It's Thursday, isn't it? I was supposed to meet with Gabe today." Laci rubbed her temples. "I have to give him a call and let him know I'm okay."

"I'm sorry, Laci, but no calls. No one can know where you are. Even your manager. It won't take the press long to figure out you're not at the hospital. And if your manager comes here, the press will follow him. They're going to be on the hunt for you."

Laci let out a big breath. "You're right. Of course. He's going to be furious."

Chapter 2

GABRIEL

GABRIEL VAN NEUGH STUFFED his frustration down, internally yelling *Where the heck is she?* He ran his hand through his black hair and blew out a noisy breath.

Laci was never late. If anything, she was annoyingly early to meetings. And this meeting was important. They were firming-up plans for her first world tour. He'd just talked to her yesterday, so he knew she hadn't forgotten. She was as excited as he was and planned on being here. What would have stopped her from coming?

Or who?

Gabriel stopped at that thought. Fear gnawed at the edges of his brain. He couldn't let himself go down that rabbit hole right now. After all, there were others in the room.

This tour was the next big step for both of their careers, and he was determined to make it happen. Not just make it happen, but make it happen *successfully*. Laci Love would be a star around the world by the time they were done. This had been their dream from the beginning. And they'd both worked their tails off to get to this point.

"Excuse me a minute, folks. I need to make a quick phone call, then we can get this meeting started." He walked out of the conference room and down the hall. He stopped at Kelly's desk, right outside his own office.

"Kelly, where is she?" he hissed.

"I've called her ten times already, Mr. van Neugh. I can't get a hold of her." After two months of asking Kelly to call him Gabriel, he'd given up.

He gave her a curt nod. "Keep trying. I need to start this meeting without her. If you hear anything, please interrupt." At her nod, he headed back to the conference room.

After wrapping up a productive meeting, Gabriel walked back down the hall and into his office. He paused at the window overlooking downtown Nashville. He loved looking out over the city that had been so good to him. Although, downtown Nashville had changed quite a bit since he and Laci moved here. It was bustling all day and night. There was music pouring out of every window and door along the strip and tourists enjoying it all.

The steel gray, overcast sky mirrored his mood. While the meeting had gone well—it was going to be an amazing tour—he couldn't get his mind off Laci.

Where the heck could she be?

His eyes followed the Cumberland River northwest to Germantown, where he lived and spent most of his downtime. He scoured the skyline, as always, trying to pick out his house, knowing he was too far away to see it. He'd chosen this view purposely. Looking to the future, he liked to think of it. The realtor had tried talking him into a bigger office space that faced the mountains in the other direction. He hadn't wanted to look at his past, just the future he and Laci had dreamed and worked for.

"Kelly," he called without turning around. "Have you tried Hank's phone?"

Gabriel didn't like Hank. To be fair, he'd never really liked any of Laci's boyfriends, but he *particularly* didn't like this one. Hank swaggered around like a peacock, acting like he was better than the average mortal because he played professional football. But that hadn't impressed Gabriel; it had just turned him off football. And even though he and Laci were good friends, Gabriel had never felt comfortable commenting on who she chose to go out with. He turned from the window just as Kelly stepped into the doorway.

"I did. He thinks Laci went away for a few days?"

"He *thinks* Laci went away for a few days? That's ridiculous." He shook his head. In the short time they'd been living together, Hank had kept track of

everywhere Laci went and who she was with. "Try him
again. Let me know when he's on the line."

Gabriel sat down at his large glass-and-steel desk.
It was pretentious and he knew it, but he didn't care.
It was his first big purchase when he and Laci finally
started making money. And now, seven years later, it
fit his style. He powered up his computer, not really
knowing what he would look for. As always, his computer opened to a music business website. It helped
him keep up with the latest gossip in his town.

But today, the headline staring back at him made
the blood drain from his face.

*Country Sweetheart, Laci Love, Rushed to Hospital
in Early Hours*

"Kelly!" Gabriel's voice didn't sound as strong as
he would have liked. He glanced through the article to
see what he could learn. Unfortunately, it was short on
details, as usual.

Kelly poked her head back into his office. "Yes,
sir?"

He waved her over and pointed to his screen.
"Have you seen this?"

Her pale face was half hidden by her long dark
hair, but her wide eyes told him she was as surprised as
he was. She put her hand over her mouth, which had
formed a perfect O. "Oh my goodness. Is Laci okay?"

He looked at her again. "Hank didn't mention
this?"

She shook her head, her face still pale, her eyes
shiny. "I got a call early this morning from a reporter

asking about Laci. I told him she was due in this morning for a meeting. I didn't know about this."

Gabriel had to figure out what was going on so he could stay ahead of the news. By the end of the day, everyone would know what he'd just learned. Hopefully, he'd soon have some answers to share.

They spent the next hour calling local hospitals, only to find none had Laci registered. Hank still wasn't answering his cell phone. Gabriel wasn't sure what to do next.

Where the heck was Laci?

He was sure Hank knew something. That was probably why he wasn't available. But where was he? He couldn't imagine what Laci saw in that guy. He was arrogant and overbearing and not even a good player. Gabriel had never been convinced he was in love with Laci, just with her lifestyle and money. Maybe he needed to head over to her house to see what was going on there.

A light tap on the door brought him back as Kelly poked her head in. "I was going to leave if you don't need anything from me, sir?"

He glanced at his watch. Five o'clock already. How did that happen? "No, go ahead. Thanks, Kelly."

"Oh, I almost forgot. Your tux was delivered from the cleaner. It's ready for the bachelor auction tonight."

Crap.

In all the confusion and worry of the day, he'd completely forgotten about the bachelor auction. Why had he ever agreed to that?

Because his good friend, Carl, had asked him to. Well, Carl's new fiancée, Grace, had asked. He'd said yes on a lark. It sounded fun, and it was for a worthy cause.

But now he really didn't want to go. But he couldn't let Carl or Grace down, so he'd show up in his tuxedo and the cowboy boots he was wearing.

He nodded. "Thanks, Kelly. Have a good evening."

Standing backstage, Gabriel scratched his cheek and realized he should have shaved before coming. *Too late now.*

"You're up in about forty-five minutes, Mr. van Neugh," one of the many assistants running around backstage informed him. "Feel free to grab a drink or something to eat in the green room. I'll find you when I need you. Don't go far." She smiled at him and was on her way.

He already had a beer in his hand, and food wasn't on his mind right now. He'd hoped to hang out with Carl but hadn't seen his friend. So instead, he stood in the wings and scouted the audience. Not surprisingly, it was 95 percent women. And most of them looked to be sixty-five or older. There were a couple faces he recognized from business. They were all having fun, and Grace's foundation was raising a lot of money to help abused women.

His eyes were drawn to a redhead in the front row. She was stunning. She looked to be about thirty, which he supposed was one of the reasons she and the auburn-haired woman next to her stood out in the crowded room. Another reason was her long, wavy merlot hair, sparkling with some sort of a pin unsuccessfully holding back the curls around her face. She wore a short black, glittery dress that hugged her curves in all the right places. The high neckline shouldn't have been sexy, but it teased his imagination.

She must have felt his stare because she turned and stared back at him. Her green eyes locked on his. He felt a prickle of interest as her gaze roamed boldly over his tuxedo. He hadn't felt that jolt in a long time. *Curious.* She raised an eyebrow at him, making him wonder if she'd felt the zing too, then she turned away to talk with her friend.

The friend looked familiar, but he couldn't place where he might know her from. That was going to bug him until he figured it out.

He watched the woman off and on for the next several minutes, waiting for his turn on stage. She ignored him, but her friend looked over a few times, which made him think they might be talking about him.

Geesh. He felt like he was in middle school again, wondering if the girl across the room liked him.

The touch on his shoulder startled him out of his thoughts. It was time. He walked behind the assistant as she explained the process, where he needed to stand, and where to go after his part was over. He nodded, even though he hadn't really heard a word she'd said.

He hoped the sexy redhead in the front row would bid on him; he hadn't seen her bid on anyone the whole time he'd been watching. He shook his head at the thought. He didn't need *that* in his life right now. Right now, he needed to find Laci and figure out what was going on. He'd stopped at Laci's house before coming here. It was empty, as expected. It didn't make it any less frustrating or concerning.

He walked on stage as Grace introduced him. He was impressed when she pronounced his name correctly—Gabriel van *New*—not phonetically, like most people did. He smiled at her and leaned down to buss her cheek with a kiss, a habit from growing up with a French father, before settling on the stool next to her.

He touched his black cowboy hat and nodded to the room of women, amused by the tittering as he gave them all a small smile. He realized he came across as the bad guy cowboy with his black boots, black tuxedo, and black hat. Several days' worth of scruff on his face helped the image. But he was one of the least known bachelors at the auction—few people knew the names of managers. The most popular bachelors for the auction were yet to come—country music stars, sports stars. They were who would bring in the big bucks for Grace.

He listened as Grace read off the details of the date he'd organized. He was pleased with what he'd come up with...with Kelly's help. A horse-drawn carriage ride from this hotel around downtown, ending at Illusion, where they would share an evening of excellent dining and magic. Then the carriage would bring them back to their cars at the hotel. He figured it would be a fun and interesting evening for both the winner and him.

He chanced a glance at the redhead sitting right in front of him. Her eyes locked on his again, and he felt the same jolt of energy run through his body. He liked that she didn't look away from his stare. She met it equally and challenged it. She smiled slowly, then whispered something to her friend. He enjoyed the buzz going through his body. It had been way too long.

Most of the bachelor dates were selling for between $5,000 and $25,000—the better the date and the more popular the bachelor, the higher the bids. He was hoping the date he'd organized would bring Grace's foundation a good chunk of money. She started the bidding at $500.

It was uncomfortable sitting in the spotlight, but he resisted the urge to squirm and smiled at each woman who bid. As expected, there was a flurry of activity right out of the gate with the over-sixty set bidding, but not the gorgeous redhead in the front row. The price quickly rose from $500 to $5,000 with five women bidding.

And still the redhead watched silently.

When the bidding got to $20 thousand, one of the women bowed out, but another jumped in to take her place. It was fun—if awkward—to watch from this vantage point. The ladies all knew each other. A few even had their husbands with them. It was good, harmless fun to raise a lot of money.

When Carl and Grace had first approached him about being part of the auction, he'd been appalled at the idea of women bidding on a date with him. The more they explained though, the more he understood it was the *date*, not him, they were bidding on, and the whole point was to raise money. While he really wanted to be looking for Laci right now, he was glad he could help the cause for abused women.

The bidding reached $35 thousand and there were three women still in the running.

$40 thousand.

$45 thousand.

He looked down at the redhead and raised an eyebrow. She gave a self-satisfied smile and his heart kicked up a beat as she raised her paddle.

Chapter 3

BREENA

B REENA RAISED HER PADDLE. "One hundred fifty thousand dollars."

The crowd gasped in unison. Breena couldn't help but giggle. She'd never actually heard a crowd gasp collectively. It was impressive. Grace handled her outrageous bid like the professional she was and, when no one challenged the offer, closed out the auction.

Breena couldn't believe she'd just bought a man for $150 thousand. A pretty good deal by all appearances. She blushed at that thought. Marilyn, she thought, was probably smiling down from heaven at how Breena was spending the money she'd left her.

He'd been watching her all evening, and it had been hard not to flirt. She was here on a mission, and she'd just accomplished the first part. She stood and made her way to the checkout table on the far side of the room. Several women smiled appreciatively at her as she walked past.

She could feel someone's gaze following her. Looking around, she found Gabe waiting for her next to the checkout table. She could feel the intensity of his gaze all the way to her toes. Butterflies started dive-bombing in her stomach.

Yikes!

What was she getting herself into? It was too late to wonder about that now, she supposed as she reached the table.

"Wow! That was awesome," the young woman working the checkout gushed.

Breena smiled at her, then taking a deep breath, stuck her hand out. "Gabe, it's a pleasure to meet you. Breena O'Malley."

"It's Gabriel, not Gabe." His warm, hard hand closed around hers.

Her breath caught in her throat as an electric current traveled from his fingers all the way up her arm. *Oh boy*, she thought. She enjoyed the delicious feeling that came with attraction, but this was more than she'd anticipated.

"I'm not sure what you expect for $150 thousand, but this should be interesting." He cocked an eyebrow at her, swagger emanating from him, even in this casual stance.

Dang, why was she always drawn to sexy, arrogant guys?

Too bad he wasn't for her. She suspected he could be a lot of fun.

"I'm expecting a good dinner and to be able to help Grace's foundation," she responded, embarrassed by how priggish she sounded, even to herself.

"No expectation of a dazzling companion?" Gabe raised an eyebrow, his deep chuckle sending a delightful shiver down her spine. "As far as food goes, you're in for a treat. The meal is guaranteed to be spectacular." He tilted his head a bit to the side. "And that was a *very* generous donation. I'm sure Grace appreciates it."

They could hear the auction going strong for the next bachelor—a charismatic Tennessee Titan football player, who seemed to be very popular with the crowd. Breena was glad to see the bids were going much higher, much quicker, for this bachelor. Maybe her ridiculous offer had set the tone for even higher bids. She finished the paperwork and payment for the donation, and she and Gabe agreed their date would be the next evening at seven o'clock.

"So I'll meet you here for the carriage ride," Gabe said, starting to leave.

"No, I'm sorry. I can't meet you here," Breena said quickly. "I need you to pick me up at my apartment."

Breena needed to get him to her apartment. Otherwise, her plan would fail, and the date would be...well, just a date. And that was not what she'd paid that exorbitant donation for.

"Excuse me?" His brow furrowed, his confusion evident. He spoke slowly, as if unsure whether she was unbalanced. "You want me to pick you up? At your apartment?"

"Oh, thank you so much." She was railroading him, and almost felt bad about it, but it couldn't be helped. "I really appreciate it."

He looked taken aback.

She knew he hadn't agreed but couldn't let that stop her. She handed him a notecard with her address. "So I guess I'll see you tomorrow night then. A little before seven? Looking forward to it." She gave him a dazzling smile, then turned and walked back to Jillian, willing her legs to not give out under her.

Part two of her plan, accomplished.

She linked arms with Jillian and steered her to the exit. As much as she'd like to stay and support Grace, she needed to get back to Laci.

"Did he agree to pick you up?" Jillian asked quietly.

"Not exactly. But I pretended he had. I'm sure he's very confused about what just happened." Breena let out a long breath. "It's probably a good thing we're not actually going out. That man could be trouble."

Thirty minutes later, the doors to the elevator quietly opened to the penthouse apartment that used to be Grace's mothers. It was colorful, warm, and homey. The only alteration they'd made was to remove the stripper pole from the middle of the living room. Carl had moved it to his house. Then he'd used the pole in his proposal to Grace on Christmas morning a few weeks earlier. It had been fun to be part of that Christmas secret.

Breena loved stepping into the apartment and seeing the colorful mirror facing the elevator. Marilyn had written *Smile* in bright red lipstick on it. Wanting to preserve it, Breena and Grace had painted clear acrylic over the sentiment. Just seeing it every time she walked into the apartment filled her heart with both love and grief.

Grace's mother had passed away the previous year after battling dementia. Breena had been one of her main caregivers. It had been a mission of love to care for the woman who had brought Breena into her home when she was nine years old and made her part of their family. And now, she and Grace were continuing Marilyn's work by helping women hide from their abusers.

Stepping into the living room, she saw Carl, Grace's fiancée, sitting on the couch with Laci. Conversation immediately stopped and they both turned around.

"How'd it go?" Laci asked. "Did you win the auction?"

Jillian let out a bark of laughter "Oh my gosh, you should have seen it."

Breena rolled her eyes.

Jillian told them the story. "The bidding was hot and heavy for the longest time. It was down to three women. The bid was $45 thousand—$45 thousand! And what does our girl do? She closes down the house with a bid of $150 thousand."

Laci stared at Breena, then burst out laughing before wincing and grabbing her ribs. "I would have loved to have seen Gabe's face."

"You mean *Gabriel*, not Gabe," Breena said in a deep voice.

Laci rolled her eyes. "He did not use that on you, did he?"

"Oh yes."

"So when is he coming?" Laci anxiously asked. This was, after all, the point of the whole plan.

"Our 'date' is tomorrow night," Breena said, using air quotes. "He is not happy about having to pick me up."

"Ha! I bet he isn't. When Gabriel has a plan, you do not mess with it. Being the workaholic that he is, I'm surprised he even agreed to participate." Laci smiled at Breena. "Thank you for doing this. I know it was a big ask."

"It was fun. We agreed it was the easiest way to get him here without raising suspicion. The timing of the auction was perfect. And the press will never suspect our 'date' has anything to do with you."

Carl looked at Jillian. "No bachelor for you, sis?"

"Ha! No. Although a few were tempting. A little out of my price range." Jillian's deep blue eyes danced with laughter. She turned to Carl. "Want a ride home? It's been a long day, and I have an early shift."

Breena hugged them both as they walked past her. "Thanks for going with me tonight, Jilly. It was fun."

"Anytime, girl. Next time though, I'm bringin' my credit card." She winked, then headed to the elevator with her brother.

"Bye Jillian," Laci called from the couch. "And, Carl, thank you for hanging out with me."

He waved his hand in response as they stepped into the elevator.

Breena went over to the couch where Laci was still sitting. "So how are you doing?" She gave her guest a once-over. "You look rested."

"Yeah, I'm afraid I slept most of the time Carl was here. Not particularly good company for him." She grinned. "While everything is still sore, I do feel better than I did this morning."

"Are you ready to tell me what happened?"

Laci took a deep breath. "I think I'd rather explain to everyone all at once. Gabe's going to demand I tell him, so how about you ask Jillian to come back to-morrow? I'd like her to take my statement at the same time."

"You want to press charges?"

"Yes." Laci nodded, her fingers lacing together. "And I want that jerk out of my home. Gabe will help with that." She paused. "I suspect Jillian can help with that too, being a cop and all."

"Jilly, I'd imagine, will be happy to help. Now, are you tired? Or would you like to watch a movie with me?" Breena asked.

She saw Laci studying her. "I think I'd like to read in bed. Is there any way I can sleep over here though? It's kind of lonely in the other apartment."

Breena knew she must look tired since she was running on two hours of sleep and appreciated that Laci hadn't brought it up. "We have a guest room next to mine. Let's get you settled in there."

Seated at the dining room table with her laptop, Breena pulled up her email to do a quick check before starting her day. Her coffee cup froze halfway to her mouth. Setting it down carefully, she took a deep breath and looked again at the email that had caught her attention.

Re: Mr. Peter Michael Simmonds

With a shaky hand, she clicked on the email to read the response Mr. Peter Simmonds had for her.

Dear Ms. O'Malley,

While it would no doubt be a delight to be your father, I'm afraid you must have the wrong man. Despite years of trying with my wife, I don't have any children.

I do remember dating a Maeve briefly in my early twenties, but I never heard from her again. I can't imagine if she was pregnant, she wouldn't have said anything.

I'm sure this isn't the response you were hoping for, but I wish you well in your search.

Best,

Peter

The sound of the coffee pot sliding into the machine brought her back to the present.

With her blonde hair sticking out in different directions and her arms gingerly wrapped around her middle, Laci sat next to Breena at the table. This was not the Laci Love fans saw in the gossip magazines, but she was still a beauty.

"You okay?" Laci reached out and covered Breena's hand. "You're crying."

Breena reached up to find her cheek damp with tears. "Oh. I didn't realize…"

Laci handed her a napkin to wipe her cheeks.

"How'd you sleep?" Breena asked, avoiding the question and closing her laptop.

"Surprisingly well. But then I rolled over wrong and…ouch!"

"Yeah, I bet that didn't feel good. How are your ribs feeling now?"

"Like I've got knives poking around in me, but otherwise great." Laci winced as she chuckled. "I keep forgetting I can't laugh."

"I'll rewrap them when you're ready." Breena felt like a mother hen clucking around, but she took her job seriously.

"I'm good for the moment, but later, I could use some help with a shower. My hair needs a good wash, and I'm not sure I can do that on my own." She laced her fingers together on top of the table. "Nothing awkward about having to ask someone to help you wash your hair…"

"I'm a nurse. It's what I do. Nothing awkward at all." Breena brushed it off. "We'll get you cleaned up and feeling better."

"And looking better, hopefully." Laci grinned. "Although, with my face being so colorful, I'm not sure that's going to happen. I don't have any clothes here either. Ugh."

"We should have you covered there. Grace picked up a few things yesterday, and we have a closet full of clothes in all sizes. We'll find something comfortable in the right size that will work for you. Oh for dinner tonight—since I'm obviously not going out, I was thinking of making something for all of us. Does ziti sound okay to you?"

Laci's stomach grumbled in response. "In case you haven't noticed, I like to eat. Speaking of..."

"I'm on it." Breena laughed. "Let's have some breakfast."

Chapter 4

GABRIEL

G ABRIEL LOOKED UP AS his office door flew open. Hank stood there, drunk and disheveled.

"Where is she, man? Where the hell is Laci?" he said as he staggered into the office.

Kelly followed on his heels, looking apologetic. She mimed calling the police with a questioning expression. Gabriel gave her a slight nod, then turned his attention to Hank.

"I was about to ask you the same question, Hank. Where's Laci?"

"How would I know where she is? She doesn't go anywhere without you knowing. I need to know where she is. I just want to make sure she's okay."

Gabriel stood up and matched Hank's stance, hands on the desk in front of him, leaning forward. Gabriel's six-foot-two frame towered over Hank by several inches. Hank was in excellent condition—he was a professional athlete after all—but Gabriel was in good shape too.

While Hank's voice kept getting louder, more frantic, Gabriel's became quieter, more menacing. "Why would you wonder if she's okay, Hank? Did you hurt her?"

The look in Gabriel's eyes had Hank staggering backward, falling into the chair behind him. "No, no. Of course not, man. We just had a fight, you know? All couples fight, right? No big deal." Hank's eyes flicked around the room. Nervous. "Just tell me where she is, man."

"What did you do to her, Hank?" Gabriel noticed police officers in the doorway but kept his focus on Hank. "Tell me, Hank, did she annoy you? Need a little roughing up?"

Hank stood up quickly and shoved everything on Gabriel's desk to the floor. "I didn't do nothin' she didn't deserve, man. Where is she?" he yelled.

The female officer tapped her stick on the door. "'Scuse me, gentlemen."

"What the hell, man? You called the cops? You called the cops on me!" Hank tipped over the chairs and threw one at the officers.

"You're going to want to settle down, sir." The officer walked calmly toward Hank. "Look, sir—"

He took a swing at her, a glancing blow to the shoulder. It was like watching a poorly choreographed dance in slow motion. Gabriel was quite sure she could have avoided it if she'd wanted to.

She put a look of mild surprise on her face. "Are you assaulting a police officer, sir?" She looked at her partner. "Mike, did he just assault an officer of the law?" At Officer Mike's nod, she pulled out her handcuffs. "I'm afraid you'll have to come with us."

"I'm not going anywhere!" Hank lunged toward the officer but was on the ground with his hands cuffed behind his back within seconds.

Gabriel just stood there, mouth gaping. He looked to the doorway where Officer Mike leaned against the frame.

"You good there, Officer Montgomery?" he called over.

"Oh, yeah. No problems here, Mike. You mind reading this nutcase his Miranda rights while I take statements?"

Officer Mike wandered over, hauled Hank off the ground with one hand, and marched him out of the office. Gabriel looked over at Officer Montgomery, then narrowed his eyes.

"Hey, I saw you at the auction last night, didn't I? You were sitting next to the redhead who won my...auction package. Breena." He hesitated to call it a date because it felt too personal.

The officer smiled and came forward, her hand out. "Jillian Montgomery," she said, shaking his hand. "It's a pleasure to meet you."

"I knew I recognized you. You're Carl's sister, right? Gabriel van Neugh. Good timing getting here. Appreciate it."

"So what happened?" Jillian nodded toward the doorway. "Who is that guy, and why was he giving you grief?"

"He's Hank Swink. Laci Love is his girlfriend." He noticed the officer's eyes go wide at that piece of information. "He was trying to find out where she is...except I don't know."

"You asked him if he hurt her. Do you think he did?"

"He's certainly capable of it. He mentioned they got in a fight and said he 'didn't do nothin' she didn't deserve.' I'm not sure exactly what that means, but the fact that he doesn't know where she is concerns me."

"Did he take a swing at you? Or just at your desk and furniture?"

"He didn't touch me. Though to be honest, I was kind of hoping he would. Impressive job taking him down, by the way."

Officer Jillian grinned. "He wasn't particularly challenging. I'd guess he's been drinking. Smelled like it and acted like it. So is Laci Love missing?"

"I'm not sure." Gabriel rubbed his hand over his face. "We had a meeting scheduled yesterday that she missed. It was important. One I know she wouldn't have skipped on purpose. I'm concerned he might have done something to her."

Officer Jillian nodded and headed out the door. "We'll get to the bottom of this. Thanks for calling us."

Kelly poked her head in as soon as the officer was gone. "You okay, Mr. van Neugh?"

"Yeah, just a big mess to clean up."

"I'm sorry he got in." She hung her head. "I tried to stop him, but he just pushed his way past me."

Gabriel's head shot up, and he narrowed his eyes. "Did he touch you? Hurt you?"

"He just sort of shoved me aside. My hip's a little sore from hitting the desk, but I'm fine." She kneeled and started picking up and organizing the papers on the floor.

"I think we need to let the police know about that."

Kelly's head came up fast, her eyes wide. "Oh no, sir. I'm fine." Her voice trembled a little.

"It might help establish a pattern of violence, might help the police put him away."

"I guess if it's necessary, I can talk to them," she said quietly.

Gabriel nodded.

"What do you mean she won't come down? We have a date." Gabriel was not completely sure how he'd been suckered into picking Breena up in the first place. And now she wanted him to go up. To meet her at her door? "Fine."

He couldn't wait until this evening was over. He knew his temper was close to the surface after his encounter with Hank, but for some reason, this woman was pushing all of his buttons.

The burly doorman got into the elevator with him, stuck a key into a slot, and pushed the PH1 button. The doors slid closed, and they made the quiet trip to whatever floor the pampered princess occupied. She seemed to live in a world where, apparently, everyone catered to her whims. Gabriel was glad he was only committed to one date.

The elevator came to a stop, and the doors silently opened. He stepped out into an entryway, only to see himself reflected in a colorful mirror. In the reflection, he watched the elevator doors close behind him. *Well, here goes nothing*.

He walked from the entryway into an empty living room. On the wall opposite, there was a large fireplace with huge picture windows on either side looking out over downtown Nashville. He could hear people talking in a different room. *Am I in the right apartment?*

Just then, Breena walked around the corner and spotted him. "Oh good, you're here" She smiled. "Hi, Gabe, come on in."

Gabriel stood rooted to the spot. "It's Gabriel," he said automatically.

He looked her up and down. He rarely commented on what his dates wore, but this was ridiculous. She had on a pair of jeans with a rip in one knee, a green sweater, and slippers. He looked again. Yes, slippers.

"I'm sorry, but you are *not* wearing that on our date. You can't. They have a dress code. I...I guess I should have mentioned that." Gabriel shook his head, feeling felt like he was in an alternate reality.

She reached out a hand. "Come with me."

It was such a simple statement, he didn't hesitate to take her hand. He ignored the flash of heat shooting through his body at her touch. He'd hoped it was a fluke when it happened the previous night when they shook hands. Apparently not.

They walked through the living room into a large combination kitchen-dining room with windows all along the far wall. It was spectacular.

Then he stopped, frozen in his tracks. Carl and Grace sat at the dining room table. Next to them was Laci. It was so unexpected to see her there, he wasn't sure how to react. He tried to lunge forward to crush her in a hug, but Breena, still holding his hand, held him back.

"Be gentle, Gabe. She's still very sore. She has a few bruised ribs."

He could feel his mouth go dry as he looked from Breena to Laci. This time, he looked her over more thoroughly, noticing the darkening around her left eye. Her swollen, deep-pink cheek. And her sweater seemed bulkier, which made him realize her ribs were probably wrapped.

He walked over and sat next to her, taking her hands in his. "How...What..." He wasn't sure where to start. "I am so happy to see you." He closed his eyes for a second holding her hands to his heart, grateful to know Laci was safe. "I need to know what happened and how you got here." He looked back at Breena. "There are so many pieces here that don't fit."

Laci leaned over and kissed his cheek. "I'm happy to see you too. It's been so hard not calling you. And I promise to tell you everything. We're waiting for one more person so I only have to tell the story once." As she spoke, Officer Jillian walked into the room. Except she wasn't in uniform. She was in jeans and a sweater.

"Sorry I'm late." She looked around. "Oh, Gabe, you're here. Did you tell her?"

"It's Gabriel," he said with a sigh. "And no. I just got here myself."

Ignoring the questioning look from the others, Jillian walked straight into the kitchen. "Breena, it smells delicious in here. I'm starving. Are we eating?" She sniffed the air appreciatively and looked expectantly at her friend.

Breena smiled. "Yes, we are. Gabe, can you help me put everything on the table, please?"

He walked over to the kitchen, noticing for the first time the scents emanating from there. Spicy tomato sauce of some sort. Garlic. His stomach rumbled, and he remembered he'd missed lunch earlier due to the altercation with Hank.

"Jillian is right—it does smell delicious in here."

"What was she talking about, 'did you tell them'?" she asked quietly as soon as he was next to her.

"I want to hear Laci's story first, then I'll share."

She nodded. "Listen...I'm sorry for all the subterfuge and that we're missing that amazing date you planned. The bachelor auction was the easiest and quickest way we could think of to get you here without the press becoming suspicious."

He gave her a curt nod. "Well, it was certainly clever."

He set the large pan of ziti in the middle of the table while Breena brought out the salad, garlic bread, and wine.

Gabriel settled into the chair next to Laci, realizing it had been years since he sat around a table with so many people. Unless they were clients. It felt oddly intimate. Uncomfortable even. Instead of dwelling on his lack of close friendships, though, he filled the wine glasses and his plate and dug into a delicious meal, letting the conversation flow around him. He could feel the tension from the last couple of days leaving his body. His shoulders relaxed and the headache that was threatening just behind his eyes was gone.

After everyone finished eating, they settled in the living room with a fire in the fireplace, ready to hear the stories. Laci started.

"Wednesday evening, I went to dinner with a friend. When I got home, it was obvious Hank had been drinking. I told him about our meeting on

Thursday, Gabe, about the world tour." She took a deep breath before continuing. "He went ballistic."

She looked across the room at him, and Gabriel knew he wouldn't like what came next.

"We'd talked about the tour before, Hank and I, so he knew we were planning it." Laci looked at her hands in her lap. "At first, he just yelled about how inconsiderate I was, only thinking about myself, never him. Then it progressed to throwing and breaking things—my things, of course. When I wouldn't back out of the tour, he accused me of cheating on him...with you."

Gabriel looked startled at this comment. He stood up and walked to the window to the right of the fireplace but kept quiet, his hands in his pockets, balled into fists. Fury roared inside him as he watched the woman who was like family to him. He needed her to continue. She needed to be able to finish her story.

"That's when he started the physical abuse." She touched her face before detailing everything for Jillian's benefit. Breena, sitting next to her, gently held her hand. "That's all I remember."

Gabriel couldn't go to her yet. His anger was still too close to the surface. He knew if he saw Hank anytime soon, he wouldn't be able to control himself. He was grateful Breena was next to her, comforting her.

Jillian spoke next. "My partner and I responded to the 911 call. When we got to the house, the kitchen door was open so we entered after announcing ourselves. The house was trashed. Broken glass all over the place. We found Laci on the floor in the living room, and we called for an ambulance to assess her injuries."

Gabriel was confused. "But if you called an ambulance, how did she wind up here?"

"Before the ambulance arrived, Laci and I were able to talk for a bit. She told me her boyfriend had hit her. When I asked if she felt safe in her house, she said no. So when I offered to stash her in a safe place, she accepted. Once the medics arrived and looked her over, we sent the empty ambulance to the hospital. We knew the press would follow it but wouldn't be fooled for long. That's when I called Bree and asked to bring her here."

Breena must have seen he was still confused because she jumped in before he could ask more questions. "This house was set up as a safe house for women by Grace's mother six or so years ago. We moved in three months ago. We decided last month to open it back up for situations that made sense. Like Laci's." She looked at Laci and smiled. "She needed care, a place to hide, and it made sense to bring her here. Very few people even know we do this, so Laci is safe. No one will find her."

Just then the buzzer startled them all. Breena answered the call to find Brian on the other end.

"Excuse me, ma'am, but I have a Mr. Hank Swink here. He demanded to speak with you. May I send him up?"

"How did he get out of jail so quickly?" Gabriel growled.

"Hank was in jail?" Laci asked.

"Well, that was *my* news to share, but it sounds like he's already out." Gabriel huffed out a frustrated breath.

Breena calmly interrupted. "Laci, you need to head next door. There's nothing of yours here, so it's okay. He won't find you. I promise."

Jillian helped Laci up off the couch.

"I'll come in as soon as it's clear. It shouldn't be long." Breena watched Jillian and Laci head off, then turned to look at the rest of the group. "Okay, Carl, would you and Grace mind putting the dishes in the dishwasher? And, Gabe, can you clear the table of all the settings, please?"

She went back to the intercom and finished with Brian. "Sure, Brian. We're just finishing a dinner party, but he can come up."

Gabriel was completely confused. He did not like the idea of Hank coming up here with Laci in the apartment. How would he not find her? And he wasn't completely sure he could trust himself not to haul off and punch the guy after all he'd just heard.

"Gabe, the silverware and glasses. Please." Breena's voice was calm but urgent.

He nodded and headed into the dining room just as the elevator doors opened.

Chapter 5

BREENA

BREENA WALKED OVER TO the elevator to meet Hank just as the doors slid open. She stumbled back a step when the scent of lavender, mint, and alcohol hit her. She was unable to stop a flood of memories from invading her mind.

She was nine years old. Her mom and her newest boyfriend were dropping her off at school. His clothing, while expensive looking, was rumpled. His hair could have used a good wash and a comb. He looked like he hadn't shaved in a day or two and smelled of alcohol and aftershave. A gross combination, she'd determined.

Her mom had acted weird all morning. Giggling at everything the boyfriend said, dropping things, forgetting Breena was in the room. Breena had seen it before. Too many times.

It was the last time she saw her mom. After they dropped her off, her mom asked Grace's mother to pick her up from school.

She shook off the memory and held out her hand. "I'm Breena. How can I help you?" She was glad to see Brian still in the entryway, arms loosely folded across his wide chest.

Hank ignored her hand and pushed past her. "Where the hell is she?"

"There are two other *shes* in the apartment." She turned toward the kitchen. "Grace?"

Grace walked into the living room, drying her hands on a towel. "Yes?"

"Who the hell is she? I want Laci. Where's Laci?" His voice was getting louder.

"Laci?" Breena looked at Grace, then back to Hank. "Laci who?"

She could see him becoming more agitated. "Laci Love. Where the hell is Laci Love?"

"Oh my gosh," Breena babbled. "I *love* Laci Love. Is she here with you?" Breena knew she was pushing it but kept up the pretense.

Just then Gabe and Carl walked into the living room. She noticed Hank stiffen

"See, I knew it. Where is she?" Spittle flew from his lips as he pointed at Gabe.

Jillian walked into the room. It was almost comical watching Hank react to each new person.

"What is *she* doing here? Did you call the cops again?" he snarled at Gabe.

Breena walked in front of Hank, dragging his attention to her. "Listen, we just finished having dinner. There is no one else in this apartment. You are welcome to look around, but if you touch anything or any*one*, I will have you arrested."

Jillian stepped forward. "I'll be happy to accompany Mr. Swick on his walk-through." She looked at him. "Shall we?"

She could tell Hank didn't understand what was going on, but he nodded at Jillian, and together, they headed in the same direction Laci had gone—through the dining room toward Breena's bedroom.

Gabe looked like he was about to ask a whole lot of questions. Breena shook her head, grabbed his hand, and led him to the couch.

"Let's get comfortable while we wait. It shouldn't take too long. This place isn't that big." She tried to transmit that everything would be okay through her expression, but Gabe still appeared anxious.

Carl and Grace walked to the couch across from her and Gabe, Carl keeping Grace snug against him, even after they sat down. While Breena was happy Grace had found the perfect guy for her, she could admit—at least to herself—she was more than a little envious. Maybe one day she'd have that kind of relationship with someone who was perfect for her. Someone she could trust to stick around. Someone who would make her a priority.

She could hear Jillian and Hank walking around at the other end of the apartment; it sounded like clothing was moved aside in the closet. A couple of minutes later, they walked past, going toward the office and master bedroom on the other side of the house. Breena could see confusion on Gabe's face but couldn't worry about it now. She stood up when Hank and Jillian returned from their investigation.

"What the hell is *he* doing here?" Hank asked, pointing at Gabe.

"Gabriel?" She looked at Gabe, then back to Hank. "He's my date. I met him last night at the bachelor auction downtown, and we decided to have dinner tonight." She looked over to Gabe again and smiled. "I have to say, this is an odd first date."

He gave her a tight smile back but didn't say anything.

Then she looked back at Hank. "Listen, it would be a dream to meet Laci Love, but as you can see, she's not here." She walked to the elevator, where Brian was waiting.

"Going down?" he asked in his deep voice.

"Yes," Breena said. "He's done here. And Mr. Swick?" She waited for him to turn around and look at her. "I expect you to leave me alone. If you bother me or my friends again, I *will* call the police."

She twisted a key next to the elevator, then turned her back as the doors closed. She let out a big breath of relief.

"Oh my gosh, that was way too close. I locked the elevator so no one can come in unexpectedly." She looked at Gabe again. "I know you have questions, but

I need to let Laci know it's clear. Want to come with me?"

He walked over and followed her through the dining room to her bedroom.

"I don't usually invite guys into my bedroom on the first date, but I guess I can make an exception." She winked at him and headed straight to the closet, pushed the clothes aside, and noticed that Jillian had stacked shoe boxes in front of the button. She grinned at Jillian's thoughtfulness, moved the boxes out of the way, and touched the little button on the ground with her toe. The panel silently slid open, and she looked back to see Gabe's mouth hanging agape.

"Yeah, that was my reaction the first time too. Come on."

They walked through the opening into the secret apartment.

"Laci," she called out, standing in the middle of the living room. " It's all clear."

Laci came through the bedroom door and rushed over to them, her face flushed, eyes wide, and breath erratic. "Oh my gosh, I was so scared he would find the button. I hid in the closet in the bedroom just in case."

"You're safe here, Laci," Breena said, taking her hand. "I told Hank if he comes back, I'll be calling the police on him. Hopefully, he won't come by anymore."

The three walked back through the sliding panel and into the living room where the others were waiting.

Breena flopped down into one of the chairs and let out a long breath. "Well, that was certainly more exciting than expected."

"I wonder how Hank found this place?" Laci asked.

"He must have followed me." Gabe said. "It's the only thing that makes sense."

An hour later, it was only Breena, Gabe, and Laci in the apartment. The others had left shortly after Laci came back in. On her way out, Jillian said she would write up Laci's statement and bring it by for her to look over and sign the next day.

Breena let Laci and Gabe talk alone in the living room. She knew they had a lot to figure out, so she stayed in the kitchen and made a fresh pot of coffee. When Laci and Gabe came in, she was drinking a cup and eating a piece of chocolate pie.

"Want some?" she asked, nodding to the pie.

"Sure." They both nodded and sat at the counter; Gabe helped Laci onto one of the stools before he sat down. Breena got to work, plating two more slices of pie, and at their nods, pouring coffee for them as well.

After she settled back on her stool, she looked at Laci. "That was brave to share your story in front of everyone. How're you doing?"

"It was hard," Laci acknowledged. "But it also felt good. I feel lighter, if that makes any sense."

Breena nodded. "I've found that a magical things happen when we share our stories. The burden of carrying them becomes lighter because we aren't carrying it alone anymore."

Laci nodded. "Yes, exactly. That's exactly how it feels."

"So did you two get everything sorted out?" Breena looked between the two.

"Well, we need to work out a way for Gabe to be able to come back here...often. We have so much we still need to discuss. I'm afraid if he keeps coming, it will become suspicious." Laci dug into the pie in front of her and moaned in pleasure. "Oh yum," she said between bites.

Gabe looked at Breena then Laci. "Well, tonight Breena told Hank we were on a date. So we could pretend we're dating, and I could come here to work with you." Then he took a huge bite of pie. His eyes widened with surprise. "This is delicious."

Breena smiled back at him, feeling her cheeks heat at the compliment.

"She made it this morning," Laci said, taking another bite. Then, looking thoughtful, she turned to Breena. "Hmm, that might work...you two dating. Breena?"

"I guess?"

Gabe looked at her. "What? You don't think it'll work?"

She shook her head. "Don't you think it would just be...kind of...weird if we started dating but never left the apartment? Usually, when people have just started seeing each other, they go out. Not stay in all the time."

Laci nodded. "Hmm, yeah, I agree." She thought for a minute. "Okay, I think the only solution is for you two to *actually* date."

Gabe choked on his coffee, and Breena's fork froze midway to her mouth. She looked at Laci, then over at Gabe, who wore a deer-in-the-headlights expression. His black hair was unruly from running his fingers through it. His piercing blue eyes were staring into hers, grasping for answers.

"Hmm," she murmured noncommittally. While the thought of dating Gabe might make her body a little tingly, she knew it was a bad idea. Just one more man who would leave her. Unease settled in her stomach with the pie.

"But I'm not interested in dating her," Gabe grumbled. He must have realized how rude he sounded, because he looked at Breena and shrugged a little. "Nothing personal."

"Thanks, champ." Breena rolled her eyes. "But don't worry, you're not my type."

He was exactly her type, but he didn't need to know that.

"No, no." Laci was trying not to laugh. Her hands holding her ribs. "Just *fake* date. I don't expect you two to really like each other. Although..." she said as an afterthought. "That would certainly be convenient." She shook her head. "But no, just go out on some fake dates. Be seen around town. Make it *look* real. That way, when Gabe does come over, it fits. No one is suspicious. Especially Hank and the media."

Gabe raised an eyebrow at Breena. "What do you think?"

Even knowing this was a bad idea, she nodded. She could second-guess herself later, but for now, she was willing to help Laci. "That could work. We obviously won't have to date forever. Just until Laci gets her situation with Hank figured out. Right? I can fake date you for a little while."

He mimed being pierced in the heart with a sword. "Thanks, Red. You're great for the ego." His eyes twinkled, sending the butterflies in her stomach back into flight. "Listen, I need to get some papers together for Laci about the tour." He looked at Breena. "I have a benefit dinner I need to go to tomorrow night. Come as my date, and I can kill two birds with one stone."

"Such a romantic." She patted her heart, laughing. "Just let me know when...and what I need to wear since I obviously didn't make a very good impression tonight." She looked down at her jeans and sweater, then smirked at him.

"Cocktail attire and I'll pick you up at six." He looked at Laci. "I'm really glad you're safe." He stood up and kissed her on the cheek, then headed to the elevator. "See you both tomorrow."

Watching him leave, Breena could feel the axis beneath her shift. She just didn't know if that was a good thing or not.

As attractive as she found Gabe, she was tired of men who used her and then moved on. But maybe knowing from the outset he would be moving on would help her keep her heart in check.

Dear Mr. Simmonds,

Thank you for responding to my email.

You certainly don't sound like the type of person who would completely write off a child from your life, which makes this so confusing.

I have quite a bit of information from the investigator, informing me how he came to the conclusion you are, indeed, my father.

Would you be willing to share a bit about your time with my mother? When did you two date? That could rule you out, if the timing is completely wrong.

Thank you,

Breena

Chapter 6

GABRIEL

S ITTING AT HIS DESK the next morning, Gabriel found it hard to focus on the paperwork in front of him. It was inconvenient, the way Breena kept slipping into his thoughts. He wasn't sure what the heck he'd been thinking, agreeing to fake date her. It was going to be a challenge to be around her so often. She was tempting. But he had a hard and fast rule about his priorities, and dating wasn't on the short list.

But there was no way around it. He needed access to Laci.

While he'd dated often enough, in all the years he'd been in Nashville, never once had anyone made him want to question his rules before. His sole focus had always been family and business, and he needed to keep it that way. No redheaded temptress was going to steer him off course.

He'd been wrong in some of his initial impressions of her. She was anything but the pampered princess he'd taken her for when he was heading up in the elevator. She also wasn't flaky. He was impressed by the way she'd handled the situation with Hank. She was calmness and beauty and had a spine of steel. He'd been ready to freak out when Hank and Jillian started walking toward the bedroom where Laci had gone, but as soon as Breena took his hand, he could feel his body relax. Her calm seeped into him.

He looked up, startled to see Kelly standing in the doorway. "Oh geez!" He put his hand over his heart. "You almost gave me a heart attack. What are you doing here today?"

"I'm sorry, sir. I was about to tap on the door to let you know I was here. I wanted to finish up some filing I didn't get to yesterday."

"You know it's Saturday, right? You don't have to come in to finish work. Especially on the weekend. I want you to be home relaxing or out playing. I'm not paying you to be here all the time." Ironic, he knew, coming from a workaholic.

"I know, sir, but I don't mind. I wouldn't have been able to relax if I left it until Monday. I won't be long." She turned to walk away but poked her head back in. "Oh, how did your date go last night? It sounded so romantic." She had a dreamy look on her face.

He stopped and looked at her. So much had happened last night, he'd forgotten he and Breena were supposed to have gone on the bachelor auction date. He'd really been looking forward to eating at Illusion, but as soon as he saw Laci, the preplanned date had completely escaped his mind. He wasn't sure what to say to explain not going there.

"Oh, we wound up eating at her place last night." He saw Kelly's eyes widen and felt his cheeks heat up. He could tell what she must be thinking. May as well get the fake dating established with Kelly. She was, after all, in his life almost daily and needed to believe the lie.

"Oh...um, nice, sir." She looked down, a smile on her face. "It sounds like you two hit it off?"

"We discovered we have a lot in common." It was the truth. Laci was certainly something they had in common. "We're going out tonight instead."

"Well, I'm happy for you. Not my place to say, but it would be nice for you to have a life outside of your business. You work too much. Sorry," she said at his frown. "Anyway, I hope you have fun tonight, sir."

She walked out of his office with a knowing smile on her face. He wanted to tell her she didn't know anything but realized whatever she was thinking about Breena and him would help the ruse.

An hour later, at home with the tour paperwork ready for Laci to look over, he found himself restless and decided a run was in order. If nothing else, Breena would help him stay in shape. He would, no doubt, run off a lot of excess energy because of her. He changed into some old, gray sweats and a long-sleeved running shirt and headed out into the dark, blustery January afternoon. Times like this, he thought it would be nice to have a dog. But he knew that was unlikely to ever happen with his schedule. It certainly wouldn't be fair to the dog.

He loved running through Germantown. As he pounded his way down the brick sidewalk, he passed the restaurant that first introduced him to the area. He'd been having dinner with a potential investor and still fairly new to Nashville.

He and Laci had shared a small condo on the east side of town then. They were working their tails off, trying to get her noticed. After that dinner, he walked around the neighborhood and decided, then and there, this was where he would settle. He loved the dark red brick buildings, the trees, and the hip vibe the area gave off. But more than anything, it just felt settled. Comfortable. Each step helped clear his mind and calm his body.

Gabriel's watch buzzed at five miles, and he immediately stopped running and turned around to walk home. He didn't particularly enjoy running but found it an effective way to stay in shape. As he walked back to his townhouse, he thought about his schedule for the next few weeks and realized there were a few industry events he could take Breena to. It would all be very public, and the press would see them together and buy into the idea of them dating.

Fortunately, he wasn't a celebrity, so interest in him and his life was minimal. He was usually only noticed when he was with Laci. But because Laci was now considered missing, at least by the public, interest in him would probably bump up until Laci was out again.

Standing in front of the mirror an hour and a half later, he decided black dress pants and dark blue dress shirt were fine for the evening. He avoided wearing suits whenever possible. Thankfully, Nashville wasn't a formal town—cowboy boots and a bolo tie meant dressed up around here.

He didn't normally take dates to industry events, so this should be an interesting evening. There would be questions about both Laci and Breena. He sighed internally, thinking life was about to get complicated. He didn't like complicated. He grabbed his black leather jacket and headed out the door.

"Hey, Jillian, you headed up too?"

Jillian and Brian were standing in front of the elevator when Gabriel walked into The Athenian. This was one of his favorite buildings downtown. He appreciated that it wasn't in the middle of the touristy hoopla. Being set off just a block or two made a difference.

He was a little embarrassed about the bouquet of flowers in his hand. Jillian raised an eyebrow but didn't say anything. He noted the paperwork in her hand. "Police report?" he asked as they stepped into the elevator.

He knew Brian was one of the few who knew about Laci being in Breena's apartment so didn't mind talking in front of him. It made him feel better knowing anyone who wanted to get to Laci would have to go through Brian. And it wouldn't be easy. Brian had the build of a wrestler. Or maybe a military guy.

At Jillian's nod, he looked at Brian. "How did Hank take leaving the building? Did he go quietly?"

Brian put his key in and punched the button. "He wasn't very happy heading down. He asked a lot of questions and isn't convinced she's not here. He'll probably be watching the place for a while is my guess."

Jillian nodded at this. "I took a walk around the neighborhood before coming in and saw him sitting in his car about half a block down. I tapped on his window and reminded him he isn't supposed to bother any of you and I'm watching him. He drove away in a huff, but Brian's right, he'll probably be back."

That gave Gabriel something to worry about. Was Laci really safe here?

As the elevator doors opened, he saw Breena standing in the living room—the sunset radiating through the windows behind her—laughing with Laci, and his mouth went dry. She wore a short dark-green velvet long-sleeved dress that hugged her curves. She'd done something with her hair that left her face open.

It confused him, the contradictory feelings running through his body. He rolled his shoulders and noted the tension he'd been feeling all day was gone. Instead, he felt tension of a different sort that seemed to show up every time he was around her, a buzzing through his body, making him hyperaware of her. A long black wool coat waited on the back of the couch, but he was grateful she wasn't wearing it yet.

Jillian walked past him and touched his arm. "I'll update Laci on Hank," she said softly.

He cleared his throat and walked in behind her. "Ladies." He nodded.

"Aw, you brought your date flowers." Laci smiled.

"Well, actually, they're for you." His face felt warm as he realized he should have brought two bouquets. It hadn't even occurred to him, since this wasn't a real date. He wouldn't bring any more flowers, he decided. Too complicated.

"Well, we'll both enjoy them." Laci brushed past his rude manners and took the flowers. She looked at Breena, who had an amused look on her face.

"There's a vase in the cabinet under the sink, Laci." Breena reached for her coat, except Gabriel beat her to it. He held it while she put her arms in, their hands briefly touching as she turned to him. He saw the confused expression on her face.

Yeah, I'm confused too, he thought.

Shaking off the feelings, Gabriel walked toward the kitchen. "Oh, Lace, here's the tour paperwork for you to look over. Make any notes you have on the contract, and I can pick it up later tonight." He set the paperwork on the dining room table, then headed back to the living room.

"Will do. And have fun, you two," Laci called from the kitchen.

Gabriel looked at Breena. "You ready?" At her nod, they headed for the elevator.

Gabriel led the way to his black Corvette in the parking garage. After opening the door for her, he hurried around to the driver's side. He loved his car, but all of a sudden it felt much too small. Breena's spicy scent surrounded him, and their arms kept bumping on the armrest. He might have to get a big SUV if he was going to survive this fake dating.

To get his mind off her scent, Gabriel mentioned Jillian had seen Hank watching the building.

"Oh boy." She exhaled. "I don't think he's going to be happy any time soon. Laci wants the locks changed on the doors of her house and wondered if that's something you can take care of for her?" At his nod, she continued, "She's going over the police report with Jilly tonight, so I don't think Hank's going to be a very happy camper in the coming days."

"Couldn't happen to a nicer guy." Gabriel gave a humorless laugh. "Monday is when Laci's housekeeper is at her house, so I think I'll work with that. Hank doesn't like to be in the house when the housekeeper is there, so I'll use that to my advantage and get the locks changed while he's out. I'll also have her pack up his things and leave them outside the gate. He doesn't have a key to the gate, so that should keep him out of her property."

He saw Breena's eyes go wide. "I'm sure that will go over well. But I think it's a good plan. Let me know if you need any help. We've got people who would be happy to help get that jerk out of her house."

The lump in his throat made it hard to talk, so he just nodded in response. It was unusual for someone he wasn't paying, or who wasn't Laci, to offer to help him. He realized how few friends—*real* friends—he had. But his career was everything. He'd worked hard to create the success he had and had no intention of losing it. A small voice inside wondered if his priorities were messed up, but it was a voice he was used to tamping down.

"Hey, she'll be okay." Breena put her hand on his arm, mistaking his mood for concern about Laci. And while yes, he was concerned for her, that wasn't on his mind at the moment.

"Thank you. And if you need anything from me to keep her safe, just ask."

She nodded and squeezed his arm, sending a warm zing throughout his body before she removed her hand.

The drive to Brentwood took about twenty minutes. He and Breena talked about the area and how she liked Nashville since she'd moved here.

"I haven't been to this area before." She was looking out the window but couldn't see much in the dark.

"You'll have to drive out here during the day sometime. It's beautiful, especially in the spring or summer when everything is green."

He pulled through an open iron gate onto a long driveway. The tree-lined path was lit, showing that even though the trees were naked of their leaves, they were still beautiful. From this vantage, you couldn't see the house, but Gabriel knew it would be coming into view shortly. He loved his townhouse in Germantown, and it was perfect for him, but this house never failed to impress. And the couple who owned it, the Marshalls, were some of the nicest people he'd worked with.

He pulled around the last curve and heard Breena catch her breath. The house—well, mansion—was magnificent. The cream stucco exterior was lit up from every angle, offering a stunning view as they drove up. It was two stories with a red tile roof that looked like it belonged in Italy. It spread out wide on both sides, with wings off each side of the house.

"Beautiful, right?" he said.

"Stunning. Just...wow."

He pulled up to the front of the house, and as soon as Gabriel stopped the car, a young man was there to open Breena's door and help her out.

"Thank you, Michael." Gabriel handed the keys and a tip to the young man, then walked over to

Breena. He put a hand on the small of her back and led her to the stairs.

"Any instructions for me?" she asked, leaning a little closer.

He glanced at her. "Nope. Just be your charming self. This is my first time on a fake date, too, so I guess we're making it up as we go." He smiled at her and noticed her frowning a little. "What?"

"I just realized, I don't think you've smiled at me before," she said thoughtfully. "You should do it more often. It looks good on you."

Her comment threw him off. He smiled all the time.

Didn't he?

He leaned down, reveling in the effect her scent had on him, his mouth almost touching her ear. "You ready?"

Chapter 7

BREENA

SHIVERS RAN DOWN BREENA'S spine. This man was a constant source of confusion—cold and dismissive one minute, setting her blood on fire the next. Her ear still tingled where his lips had been.

She took a deep breath and nodded to Gabe that she was ready, straightening her back as they walked up the stairs. While she appreciated his hand on her back, steering her in the right direction and lending support, it was very distracting. The spot his hand touched was alive with nerves.

Breena had spent the majority of her life living either below the poverty line with her mother or solidly middle class with Grace's family. This kind of wealth was intimidating. It wasn't until the last few months she'd had more than enough money, and that had been a gift from Grace's mother.

Marilyn hadn't lived extravagantly and never mentioned the money before her death. She'd left the bulk of her wealth to Grace, of course, but the townhouse in Orlando where Breena and Grace had grown up was left to Breena and sold for just over a million dollars. That, combined with the cash Marilyn left her, had made Breena a rich woman.

But this was a whole different level of wealth.

A gentleman at the front door took their coats and guided them through the house. The interior was even more beautiful than the exterior. The entryway walls were white; to the left, a staircase curved its elegant way to the second floor, and to the right were three arched doorways leading to a large sitting room with a fireplace. Breena and Gabe followed the man through to the courtyard out back.

"The bar is set up in the outdoor dining area, sir."

Gabe smiled and nodded. "Thank you, Charles."

It was a chilly January evening, and Breena was grateful her dress had long sleeves. They walked down a covered breezeway toward the outdoor dining room. Off to her left, she noticed a tent on the lawn with what looked like living room chairs in groupings. Heaters were scattered around the tent to keep the guests comfortable.

Further out in the lawn, she could see fairy lights in many of the trees and a lit pathway leading into the darkness. She imagined in the summer, this was a gorgeous yard. The outdoor dining room ahead of them was a large covered space with a kitchen to one side and several dining tables seating six or eight. The ceiling of the space was covered with more twinkling lights, creating a festive atmosphere.

There had to be at least a hundred people milling about, all looking beautiful. Breena quickly realized she was one of very few who wasn't wearing black.

"Why didn't you tell me I should wear black?" she whispered to Gabe.

He looked down at her, clearly confused. "What? Why would you have to wear black?"

She rolled her eyes. He was such a guy. "I'm the only woman here *not* wearing black. I stand out," she hissed.

"No, you stand out because you're the most beautiful woman here."

She stopped and gaped at him.

"Come on, sweetheart." He grabbed her hand. "Let's get a drink from the bar."

Sweetheart?

Oh, right. He'd switched into fake dating mode. It was hard to keep up. She let out a big breath and smiled up at him.

"Sure, honey, I'd love a drink." She switched on her own fake dating mode and followed him into the crowd. She enjoyed the feel of her hand in his as they made their way to the bar. They were stopped at least a dozen times by people who knew Gabe or who he needed to say hi to.

"Gabriel, you sly fox. I didn't realize you were bringing a date tonight." A woman who appeared to be in her early sixties stopped them.

"Mrs. Marshall, a pleasure, as always, to see you." He leaned down and kissed her cheek. "Breena, may I present our hostess, Mrs. Gigi Chiapini-Marshall. Mrs. Marshall, this is my lovely date, Breena O'Malley."

Mrs. Gigi Chiapini-Marshall was the epitome of class. Her chic black pantsuit was well-made but understated. Her diamond earrings and bracelet were real but, again, understated. She had short blonde hair, and Breena suspected she had a little help keeping the color.

"It's a pleasure to meet you, Breena—" She stopped, her eyes twinkling, a big smile spreading across her mouth. "Wait a minute. I remember you from the auction. You're the vixen who outbid me on our Gabriel here."

Breena could feel her eyes grow wide. "Oh..." Noticing Mrs. Marshall's laughter, she turned to Gabe, checking him out from head to toe, then back to Mrs. Marshall. "Can you blame me?" She grinned when Gabe's neck grew a little darker around his collar.

"Not one bit, honey. Why, if I were thirty years younger and not married, well..." She winked at Breena and gave her a knowing look. "You two enjoy your evening. Oh and, Gabriel, I think Tom was looking for you earlier. You might want to hunt him down."

He nodded, and they continued toward the bar.

After finally emerging with a couple of glasses of wine, they continued their tour of his associates. Breena relaxed into the evening. She enjoyed talking with people, so hearing stories about Gabe made for a fun evening. For her, anyway.

"I don't understand why everyone thinks you want to hear stories about me," he grumbled.

"Oh, honey." She laughed. "They just want me to know the Gabriel they know. It's sweet."

He rolled his eyes. "I think I see Tom on the other side of the lawn. Do you mind if I head over there for a few minutes? You okay by yourself for a bit?"

"Sure. I'll make my way back to the bar for another glass of wine. Would you like one?" At his nod, they headed in opposite directions. She thought the trip to the bar would be quicker this time since she didn't have Gabe with her, but she was stopped only halfway across the room.

"You're with Gabriel, aren't you?" The woman was tall with white hair and was in her sixties, maybe seventies. If Breena thought her emerald-green dress stood out, it was only because she hadn't seen this woman yet. She was a sight to behold in silver-white pants, a long-sleeved silver shirt with fringe along the underside of the sleeves and sequins down the neckline, which scooped into a low V. To top it all off, she wore white cowboy boots with sparkly silver toes.

"Oh, um...yes, ma'am. I'm with Gabriel."

"Darling, I'm Tessa Starr." She stopped speaking and seemed to expect a reaction.

"A real pleasure to meet you, Ms. Starr," Breena said.

That seemed to be the appropriate reaction because the woman gave a little nod, then continued, her voice husky and a little gravely. "I have to say, it's about damn time that boy got himself a good woman. Darling, I have a proposal for your young man. Could you please have him stop by after he's done talking with Tom?"

"Of course. I'm happy to let him know you're looking for him."

"Very good." She nodded again. "I think you two might need to come to my house." She seemed to be talking to herself because she walked off before Breena could answer.

Breena stood there for a second, taking in the odd encounter. She needed to look up Tessa Starr to see who she was. There *had* to be an interesting story behind this woman.

After finally making her way to the bar, Breena put in her order with the bartender and turned around to watch the room.

"You are my hero."

Breena looked around. "Excuse me?" She focused on the blonde next to her. Tall, thin, looked to be in her mid- to late-twenties. She looked like she could be a model. Or a trophy wife. Either possibility worked with this crowd.

"What did you have to do to get Gabriel to bring you to a work function?" At Breena's confused look, she continued. "You *are* with Gabriel, right?"

"Yes, I'm with Gabe, but I'm not sure I understand the question. He asked me to come tonight. So I came."

"Gabe? He lets you call him Gabe?" A brunette next to the blonde piped in. They both raised perfectly shaped eyebrows in surprise.

The blonde spoke again. "He's never brought a date to one of these events."

The brunette nodded in agreement. "Never. He's always all business. And he never drinks anything and never stays very long."

"Hmm, I'm not sure what to tell you." Breena found it curious these two women paid so much attention to Gabe; they knew what he did and who he was with. She grabbed her two wine glasses from the bar, nodded at the ladies, and headed to the other side of the patio, away from the bar.

She knew the reason Gabe brought her here—to establish a relationship so he could come see Laci. It didn't matter what some sexy blonde or her friend thought. Though if she were being honest, even if Laci weren't in the picture, Breena would be attracted to him. His arrogant attitude warred with the kindness he showed Laci. Which, again, made her wonder about their relationship.

Settling in at a small high table near a heater, she felt someone watching her and scanned the room until her eyes collided with Gabe's. He was across the yard, still talking to Tom, but his gaze stayed on her for several seconds before he turned back to his conversation.

That man was confusing.

Chapter 8

GABRIEL

"I'm sorry, Tom, could you repeat that?" Gabriel was having a hard time focusing on this conversation. He kept losing track of Breena in the crowd. She'd been right earlier; she did stick out in this crowd. Not only because her sexy green dress wasn't black, but also because of her wavy red hair. He would love to get his hands in her hair.

"You're distracted tonight." Tom's eyes followed Gabriel's. "Understandable. She's beautiful." He winked and repeated his question.

"Oh no," Gabriel said a little too quickly. "I mean, yes she's beautiful. But..." He let his words die out. He was supposed to be convincing people he was dating her.

This was proving to be more challenging than expected.

When he'd seen Breena at the bar talking with Bunni and Teri, it was all he could do to not walk over there and drag Breena away from them. He didn't need her hearing any stories from Bunni. Or Teri, for that matter. He'd dated Bunni, very briefly, several years ago. She'd been on the hunt for a husband, preferably a rich, well-connected one. She had dreams of being a country music star, but unfortunately for her, she didn't have the talent to go along with those dreams. But she'd eventually found her rich, well-connected husband and enjoyed being the wife of a mover and shaker in the country music world.

Gabriel dragged his attention back to Tom, and they finished up their conversation. He was glad he'd tracked him down. Tom would be a key investor in Laci's world tour and Gabriel was grateful for it. He liked working with people he knew and respected. Laci would be thrilled to hear this news.

Heading to the last spot he'd seen Breena, Gabriel panicked when he didn't find her. She wasn't by the bar or in the tent. Where could she have gone? He felt tension creeping back into his shoulders as he wandered around, eyes peeled for his redhead.

Well, not *his* redhead.

Mrs. Marshall sidled up to him and hooked her arm through his. "Was your meeting with Tom worth being away from your lovely young lady?"

He looked at her and smiled. "I am very pleased we'll be working together. I appreciate your support." His eyes were still scanning the patio.

"Well, we're pleased to be able to do it, Gabriel. I'm sorry Laci's not here tonight, but I like her replacement. Is Laci okay? There are some curious rumors going around."

"Yes, Laci is fine. Don't believe everything you hear." He knew he shouldn't say anything about Laci while here and had successfully avoided doing so throughout the evening, but he wanted to alleviate the worry he saw in Mrs. Marshall's eyes.

She smiled at him. "Oh, and you might want to head that way to rescue your young lady."

He looked to the right, where Mrs. Marshall was pointing. He saw a group of men but not Breena. And then one of the men moved his head slightly to the right, and Gabriel saw her. Laughing. She lit up the night. But what were all those guys doing around her? He knew them, of course. They were all players. They enjoyed all the beautiful young women their jobs attracted. And they took full advantage of the situation whenever they could. Mrs. Marshall was right; he needed to rescue her.

"Excuse me, Mrs. Marshall. I..." He looked down and saw her knowing smile. It wasn't worth trying to explain the situation, so he nodded and headed toward Breena.

"Well, there you are, sweetheart." He worked his way into the group and slid his arm around her. He dipped his head. "I missed you." Her spicy scent surrounded him, and his body relaxed in response.

Breena turned and looked up into Gabriel's face. Their lips almost collided. He took a quick step back but kept his arm around her.

"Well, hey there, handsome."

Then he looked around, as if just now noticing the men around her. "Oh, hey guys. How are you tonight?" They all grumbled an answer before heading off to the bar. He looked back down at Breena.

"Were they bothering you?"

Her laugh surprised him. He thought she would be grateful.

"No, they were fine."

"I know those guys, Breena. They're players. They troll any new woman they see. Take advantage of single women."

"Hmm, I see. So they were only talking to me because they thought I was a naive, young woman?" She looked at him and shook her head. "Gabe, I've been single for thirty-two years. I know how to handle men. But thank you for trying to rescue me." She kissed his cheek.

Completely thrown off, his hand involuntarily went up to his cheek. It was warm where her lips had touched. Not only had she laughed at the fact that he was trying to be helpful, but she'd kissed him. This woman was confusing. And frustrating.

Breena took a small step back, putting a little breathing room between them. "Oh, I was told to give you a message. Ms. Tessa Starr needs to talk with you before you leave."

"So you met Ms. Starr, did you?" He grinned. "She's a legend around here. Let's go see what she wants from me." When he grabbed Breena's hand, he realized he was starting to enjoy the heat that went up his arm whenever they touched. "What'd you think of our Ms. Starr?"

Breena stuck close to him as they wound their way through the crowd. "She's...something," she said noncommittally.

He laughed at that.

They found the legend holding court in one of the chairs under the tent, a small group of admirers around her. As Gabriel stepped into her circle, she shooed away the crowd so she could speak with them.

"Ah, I see your lovely young lady gave you my message. Well, Gabriel, what do you think? Will we be working together?"

"Hmm?" Gabriel looked at Breena, who looked confused. "It's a pleasure to see you, Ms. Starr." He leaned down and pecked her cheek, then pulled a couple of chairs next to her and settled in for the conversation. "Now, since Breena doesn't work for me, I'm expecting you'll share the details with me of what you want to do together."

Gabriel knew from experience you couldn't assume you knew what Tessa Starr wanted. It was best to let her spell it out.

"Well, aren't you the crafty one?" She barked out a laugh. "I have some young artists who would be perfect for that world tour you're organizing."

He'd learned long ago Tessa Starr was, without a doubt, the best connected woman in Nashville. It didn't pay to wonder where she got her information. He also knew her instinct about up-and-coming artists was on point.

"How about you send me some tracks? I'd love to hear who you've got."

She winked at him. "It arrived at your office this afternoon. Let me know which ones you like."

And just like that, they were dismissed.

"Are you done here?" he asked Breena after they left Ms. Starr.

"Hey, I'm just along for the ride. You done?" She grinned at him.

He grabbed her hand and headed into the crowd. "One quick goodbye, then we're outta here."

He found Mrs. Marshall and waited while she finished up a conversation with a woman. He leaned down and gave her a peck on the cheek. "Thank you again, Mrs. Marshall. It's been a pleasure, as always."

She smiled up at him, eyes sparkling. "I saw Ms. Tessa corner you. She's always got something in the works. It was good to see you, Gabriel. And bring this one back. I'd like to see her again." She nodded toward Breena. "Good night, dear." She touched cheeks with Breena in an air kiss.

Breena smiled. "It was a lovely night. Thank you."

It had been a successful night of fake dating, Gabriel thought. They'd seen and been seen, so now he could visit Laci without worry. Maybe they wouldn't have to go out anymore. It would certainly make his life easier.

Chapter 9

BREENA

Dear Ms. O'Malley,

I'm happy to share what I can remember about my time with your mother. It was a brief relationship and so many years ago though.

I had to do a little googling but was able to backtrack to determine the time we went out would have been end of June/beginning of July in 1989. We went on a couple of dates, then spent a couple of nights to-

gether when we went to a Bon Jovi concert in Akron.

After that, I didn't see or hear from her again.

I hope that helps,

Peter

"**Y**OU SURE YOU DON'T mind me taking off for an hour or so?" Breena was nervous about leaving Laci alone, but Gabe was having the locks changed in Laci's house, Jillian was at work, and Grace and Carl were at their wedding cake tasting this morning.

"I'm fine. Don't be a mother hen." Laci grinned. "Brian is downstairs to stop anyone from coming up, and I'll lock the elevator. Just have Brian buzz me when you're back, and I'll unlock it for you."

After a quick, gentle hug, Breena headed down to the garage. She loved her sporty little car—red hot and fast! It was another gift from Marilyn. She'd enjoyed riding in Gabe's sporty little car on Saturday night too. She wondered if he'd be surprised to see what she drove. She shook her head. It didn't matter what he thought about what she drove.

She thought about the email she'd received that morning from Peter Simmonds. Such a short message, but it had the potential to be life-changing for both of them.

She'd looked up the concert they went to out of curiosity. Bon Jovi was a hot ticket in 1989. She remembered her mother being a big Bon Jovi fan. There was a very brief window when her mother was fun and attentive. They would have dance parties before bed that usually included a Bon Jovi song or two. Boy, she hadn't thought about those days in a long time.

She'd looked Peter Simmonds up on Google to see if there was anything about him online. He was different from what she'd expected. She'd always pictured her father as a loser, a man who was probably in prison, or at least, in and out of the system. But this man seemed like a decent guy. It had never occurred to her that her father might not even know she existed. It changed so much of how she thought of her life. She'd let her childhood, her relationship with her mother, her mother's relationship with men steer how she saw the world and her own relationships with men.

She looked around, surprised to find her car already at the parking lot for the Happy Valley Assisted Living Home. She didn't remember the drive, her mind had been so preoccupied.

After getting settled in Nashville, she'd decided since she didn't need to go back into nursing, but she wanted to spend time volunteering. She'd found Happy Valley by accident. A chance meeting at the grocery store led to an opportunity to volunteer.

Her first time here, she'd met and hit it off with a young woman named CeeCee. They'd gone for a walk around the beautiful property, painted the young woman's fingernails, and listened to music. It was a fun way to spend her time, and she really enjoyed CeeCee's enthusiastic personality. She'd even picked up a few new fingernail polish bottles in fun colors for their visit today.

Breena admired the grounds of the home as she walked to the door. As an expensive private facility, she knew the families of the residents paid heavily for the extras that came with a place like this. And if you had the means, this was certainly a beautiful place for those who needed the care provided.

After checking in at the front desk, she inquired after CeeCee and was directed to the television room on the second floor, where she found CeeCee sprawled on the couch with the television on a morning talk show. Breena was a little surprised she was watching a show that was usually full of drama and adult language. While CeeCee was probably around twenty, her brain injury had left her mentally closer to an eight- or ten-year-old. This show didn't seem appropriate for that age, but maybe the family was fine with it.

"Hey, CeeCee." She squatted by the couch. "How are you today?"

"Hi, Bee." A big smile lit up her sweet face. CeeCee was dressed in jeans and a sweater but had slippers on her feet. "I'm bored. The TV is boring."

Apparently, no one had come around to change the channel, and CeeCee didn't know where the remote was.

Breena got up and turned off the television, then walked back to her. "Well, I'm here now, so let's go for a walk. It's really nice outside." They went back to CeeCee's room to change her slippers for athletic shoes and to grab a jacket. Breena loved how chatty her young friend was. She told her all about her day so far—who she talked to, what she had for breakfast, what aides helped her this morning, and so on.

"Oh, and my brother came by." The smile on her face was even bigger when she mentioned her brother.

"How nice. Does your brother come often?" Breena asked.

"He does. He loves me and visits every week," CeeCee gushed.

Breena smiled at that. She was happy to hear CeeCee had family visiting on a regular basis. So many people didn't have anyone.

"Do you have a boyfriend, Bee?" She took Breena by surprise with her question.

"Um, no. No, I don't. Do you?"

CeeCee giggled. "No, but I think my brother should be your boyfriend."

Playing along, Breena asked. "Well, is he tall, dark, and handsome?"

"He is." CeeCee was wide-eyed that Breena seemed to know about her brother.

"Well, he's probably a little young for me, but I hope I get to meet him sometime. Ready to get going?"

They spent the next hour walking around the grounds together, listening to Taylor Swift, and painting CeeCee's fingernails purple when they got back to her room. Before she left, Breena walked CeeCee to the dining room so she was ready for lunch, then headed back to the penthouse.

"Welcome home. How was your morning?" Laci was stretched out on the couch with a book. She had on leggings and a large zip-front sweatshirt. Her long blonde hair was pulled up in a high ponytail. She looked like she was about twenty years old. Her eye was in the ugly purple-green bruise phase, but otherwise, she was looking better.

"Actually, it was a lot of fun. I volunteer at an assisted living facility. Today, I hung out with a sweet young lady. We went for a walk, listened to Taylor Swift, and painted her fingernails. She wants to set me up with her brother." Breena laughed. "How about you? What have you been up to?"

"I've just realized how little downtime I've had the last few years. I haven't napped so much in a long time. It feels good to have time to read a book."

"Your body must need rest."

"I was wondering if you have a notebook I could use? I had some lyrics come to me today, and I'd love to write them down. It's been a while since I've been inspired to write. It feels really good to have the space to be creative."

"I saw a notebook in the office. Hang on a sec." Breena headed off and was back in a minute. "Here you go." She handed Laci a beautiful leather journal and pen.

"Oh perfect, thank you."

Breena went to the kitchen and pulled out bread, ham, and cheese. "I was going to make some sandwiches and a salad. Interested?" Breena loved that Laci already had the notebook open and was writing.

"Sorry?" Laci looked up. "Yes, I'd love some lunch. Don't feel like you have to wait on me though. I feel like I'm taking advantage of you."

Breena smiled at her. "I'm happy to take care of you while you're here. It's what I'm here for. You'll be out in the cold, cruel world, fending for yourself soon enough. Enjoy it while it lasts."

Laci grinned. "You're right about that. I don't have anyone waiting on me back at my house." She stopped, looking worried. "I wonder how it's going for Gabe today, getting the locks changed."

Breena nodded. "I was wondering about that too. I'm sure you'll hear from him soon."

The buzzer startled Breena and Laci, who were both stretched out on the couch, napping.

Breena was the first up. She yawned and stretched her arms over her head, trying to get her hair into some semblance of order. "Oh my gosh, that felt so good." She walked over to the intercom. "Yes?"

Brian's deep voice came through the speaker. "Ma'am, I have Mr. van Neugh here, wondering if he can come up?"

Breena looked at Laci, who sat up, alert. "Sure, send him up." She unlocked the elevator and went back to the couch.

A few minutes later, Gabe walked through the elevator doors and into the living room. "Afternoon, ladies. How's your day been?"

"Well, I've been on the couch all day. But I did get a new song written, so I feel accomplished." Laci smiled at him.

"A new song? That's great." He looked at Breena. " And you?"

"I did some volunteer work at an assisted living facility and..." She stopped speaking because he walked right past her to sit next to Laci on the couch. Laci looked between the two of them but then turned her attention to Gabe. He set a bag on the table in front of them.

Breena had let herself forget for a minute that "attentive" Gabe was only when they were on a fake date. Grace came out of her bedroom and sat next to Breena.

"Okay, Lace, locks are changed. I sent the housekeeper home as soon as it was done. I didn't want Hank messing with her to try to get to you." Gabe said.

"Thank you for taking care of that. I know it's not part of your job, but I really appreciate it. And I really like knowing that man doesn't have access to my home any longer."

"Might not be part of the manager job, but it falls firmly into the friend job description. Oh, I forgot to mention Saturday night when I dropped off Breena, I ran into Ms. Tessa at the Marshalls."

A smile lit up Laci's bruised face. "How is she?"

"Same as ever."

Laci looked at Breena. "What did you think of Ms. Tessa Starr?"

"She definitely rocks that legend vibe." Breena laughed. "But dang, she was intimidating."

Laci grinned. "Sounds about right. I remember the first time I met her." She shivered for effect. "Scary!"

"Wait." Grace stood up quickly, her face unreadable. "Tessa Starr? The country singer from back in the '80s and '90s?"

"Yeah." Gabe nodded. "You know her?"

Grace slowly sat back down. "My mom knew her," she said quietly. "I found one of Mama's diaries—she talked about meeting Tessa Starr when she first came to Nashville in 1989. She's the one who gave Mom those turquoise boots I love so much."

"Marilyn knew Tessa Starr?" Breena looked at Grace, stunned. "Wow. I suppose I shouldn't be surprised. They're like two peas in the same closet." She chuckled.

"From what I've seen, she hasn't changed much over the years," Gabe said to Grace. He turned back to Laci. "She gave me some tracks for you to listen to for the tour. There were three bands I really liked, but I want your opinion." He opened the bag he'd brought, took out a CD player and a stack of CDs, and set them on the table.

Grace laughed. "CDs?"

Laci grinned. "She's old-school." She turned to Gabe. "I'll listen to them tonight. That woman definitely has an ear for the talented and the interesting. Might be fun to have some fresh talent on this tour. I can't wait to see how it comes together."

Gabe paused before changing the subject. "You know tomorrow will be a media storm, right? The news of Hank getting kicked out, the gates being locked, and the police report will all hit. We need to be careful and keep you out of sight. I know you can handle the media, and your bruised face would certainly gain the sympathy vote, but Hank seems to be a loose cannon right now. I'd rather have him take it out on me than you."

"Yeah, the police report is going to be a bit of an explosion." Laci leaned back and closed her eyes for a moment before continuing. "Jillian said she would try to protect the pictures from leaking, but I expect they'll get out. Hank's not going to be welcome around here much longer. This might even affect his football contract. I can't imagine this ending well for him. I was careful about what he had access to financially. His name isn't on anything, so at least that shouldn't be an issue. Though I'm sure he'll try to send me some bills."

"Okay. I'll touch base with your accountant and make sure any bills from Hank are rejected."

"Thank you."

Gabe stood up to leave then looked over at Breena. "We should probably go out again."

Breena shook her head. "It's hard to believe you're still single. You're so romantic."

He stared at her for a second. "You available for dinner tomorrow? I thought we'd go downtown, to one of those trendy spots. You know, see and be seen."

She nodded. "That works. And you're right, we probably should be seen out, especially with all the news tomorrow."

They arranged the details and Gabe left.

Breena turned to Grace. "I can't believe your mom knew Tessa Starr."

Laci sat forward in her seat. "What did your mom say about Ms. Starr? I don't know much about her early years. It's amazing your mom knew her."

"I think Ms. Starr introduced Mom to the Opry. I'm not sure what all their relationship was beyond that. I'll have to keep reading her journals."

After Grace left to meet Carl, Laci settled at the kitchen counter while Breena started dinner.

"Not that it's any of my business," Breena said, "but why *doesn't* Gabe have a girlfriend or wife?"

Laci shook her head. "Girl, don't go falling for that one. That man has only two priorities—his family and his work. He's in a *very* committed relationship with his work. Which is great for me, since he's my manager, but he makes zero space in his life for anything or anyone else. I don't think he knows what a balanced life is." She took a long drink of the water in front of her. "Who knows? Maybe for the right woman, he'd be willing to make time and space," she added, almost as an afterthought.

"No, no." Breena shook her head. "Not interested. Just curious."

Laci gave her a look that said she didn't completely buy that answer, but she didn't say any more about it. "So what about you?" Laci asked. "No love in your life?"

"Oh no. If my mother taught me anything before she abandoned me, it's that I can only count on myself. Well, myself and Grace. Men might be good for some fun, but that's about it. Besides, I was pretty much married to my job too. I was a traveling nurse for several years. Moving every year or so doesn't really encourage relationships."

Laci opened her mouth, then closed it again. "Are you going to stay here in Nashville?"

Breena wondered what her first comment had been. "I think so. I hope so. I really like it here. People are friendly, and it's beautiful. I love the mountains and the seasons. So different from Florida."

"Hmm, well maybe your love-life outlook will change now you're staying put."

"I'm not banking on it. And it certainly won't be with Gabe, right?" It came out harsher than intended, but thankfully, Laci didn't react. Breena didn't want a relationship with him. At least, not a long-term one.

She rubbed her chest to loosen the ache. The memory of her mother leaving her because of a man always made her think twice before jumping into a relationship.

Dear Mr. Simmonds,

Based on your email, the timing would be about right.

My mother made a comment once that I was conceived during "You Give Love a Bad Name." I never paid much attention to it, but now I wonder.

She also said several times that I was so impatient that I couldn't even wait forty weeks to be born.

My birthday is March 17, 1990, just under thirty-seven weeks after the concert.

I understand you probably don't need this type of interruption in your life right now, but would you be open to DNA testing?

Hopeful,

Breena

Chapter 10

GABRIEL

THE MEDIA STORM THE next day was as expected. Gabriel spent Monday morning buried under phone calls and emails. Questions about the police report. Inquiries as to where Laci was. Thankfully, Kelly fielded a lot of the calls and could honestly answer she didn't have any idea where Laci was. But since answers weren't forthcoming, speculation was ripe. All sorts of theories were tossed around as to what happened to Laci.

Midway through the morning, Hank showed up, banging on the locked door, yelling in the hallway.

"Head into my office," Gabriel instructed Kelly. "Lock the door until I let you know he's gone."

Only after she'd closed and locked the door behind her did Gabriel unlock and open the main office door.

Hank stormed in, reeking of alcohol and sweat. "Where the hell is she, Gabriel? She had me arrested, then locked me out of our house."

"From what I saw of the police report, I don't blame her for changing the locks." Gabriel gave him a pointed look. "If you were arrested, why are you here and not in jail?"

Hank gave him a blank look. "I posted bail. But I need to get into my house."

"You're talking about *Laci's* house. It seems you're not welcome if she locked you out."

"Oh, she'll let me in." This was the cocky Hank who Gabriel knew and despised. Always overly confident of Laci's feelings toward him. But this time, things had changed. For Laci, at least.

He wondered when Hank was going to realize it. "Why would she let you in, Hank? You beat her."

"It wasn't that bad. Besides, she loves me."

Gabriel wasn't typically a violent man, but it was all he could do not to punch the guy in his face. His hands kept clenching and unclenching at his sides.

"It *was* that bad, according to the police report and the pictures. You're going to need to find somewhere else to live, Hank. You are *not* going to be bothering Laci." Gabriel ground out the words through clenched teeth. There is no way Hank would be allowed back in that house. Not while Gabriel was around.

"That's not your call, man," Hank sneered.

"No, it's not. It's Laci's. And she made the call when she had you thrown in jail and changed the locks. You don't see that as an answer? She doesn't want you in her house, Hank. And if you try to go near her, I'll call the cops." Gabriel stood up, fists on desk, hoping Hank would take a swing at him so he'd have an outlet for his anger.

Just then, there was a tap on the open door. Officer Jillian stood there with her partner. Gabriel wondered if she had really good instincts or if Kelly had called them. Either way, their timing was perfect.

Hank looked back, startled. His face went pale. "You called the cops on me? Again?"

"Hank, I've been standing here talking to you for the last ten minutes. Did you see me call the cops?" Seeing Hank nervous calmed Gabriel. He sat down in his chair.

Jillian stepped forward. "I told you I would be keeping an eye on you, Mr. Swick. You didn't believe me?"

Hank's eyes went wide and sweat beaded on his upper lip. He ran his hand through his greasy hair, his gaze darting between the cops in the doorway and Gabriel.

"I also told you to stay away from Laci and her friends. You must *want* to go back to jail, Mr. Swick. Did you enjoy it last night when you were there? I'm pretty sure we could make the case for no bail this time...right, Mike?"

Officer Mike leaned against the doorframe, his arms crossed loosely over his chest. "Absolutely, Jillian. I would expect any judge would agree to no bail on this one."

Gabriel had no idea whether they were just yanking Hank's chain or not, but their words had a powerful effect. He looked like he was about to pass out—pale, sweating, and close to hyperventilating. It wasn't a pretty picture.

"How about if I just leave now? No harm done," he offered, putting his hands up in front of him in a gesture of peace.

"And where are you going, Mr. Swick? How about we drop you off?" Jillian offered.

"No, no. That's not necessary. I'll just leave, and I won't come back." He was shaking his head, looking very flustered. The overly confident man from a few minutes earlier was gone.

"Give us an address, and we'll drive you there. Otherwise, Mr. Swick, it's back to jail we go."

"What about my car? I've got my car here. It has all my belongings in it since that—" He stopped here, seeming to rethink his word choice. "Since Laci locked me out of our house," Hank whined.

Officer Mike walked into the room. "I tell you what, Mr. Swick. We'll just follow you to wherever you need to go." He took Hank's arm and led him out the door, Jillian following behind them. She turned at the doorway and winked at Gabriel before heading out.

Later that evening, Gabriel and Breena waited for their drinks in one of the trendiest restaurants in Nashville. He typically hated these types of places and avoided them at all costs—they were noisy, crowded, overpriced—but tonight was about being seen.

So here they were, at The Chew, being seen.

"Man, I love Jilly," Breena said upon hearing the conclusion of Gabriel's story about Hank. "Where did they take him?"

"I'm not sure. I didn't have a chance to follow up, but I will tomorrow. It took up my whole day, trying to stay ahead of all the gossip. It's going to be a week of long days, but I'll be damned if I let Hank ruin my business or Laci's career. I mean, I wouldn't be here with you if they weren't important, right?"

Breena's head jerked up, a frown on her face. He decided it was time to shift the focus and let her do some talking.

"So how was your day?"

"My day was pretty good..." she started.

Before she could go any further, Gabriel's phone rang. He looked at the number and excused himself. He stepped outside for a few minutes to take the call. It was a newspaper with questions about Laci and the abuse charges against Hank. He answered what he could and told them to contact the police.

Heading back in a few minutes later, he saw Breena sitting at the table, chatting with the waiter. It struck him again that Breena was a beautiful woman. Her green eyes sparkled in the candlelight. Her red hair was down and gorgeous. She looked up at him and smiled as he sat back down.

"Everything okay?" she asked.

"Yeah, sorry about that. The press is trying to figure out what's going on with Laci. I told them they needed to talk to the police, since I don't know anything." He grabbed his wine glass and settled back in. "Now. You were getting ready to tell me about your day."

"I gave my *guest* a checkup today. She's healing nicely," she said in response to his questioning look. "Then I spent the day baking. We have four loaves of homemade whole wheat bread and six dozen cookies. Happy to share if you want when you take me home."

"What kind of cookies?" he asked. Not that it mattered—he wanted homemade cookies regardless, but he was curious.

"Chocolate chunk."

"Nuts?"

She frowned slightly. "No. Why would I ruin a perfectly good chocolate chunk cookie with nuts?"

He let out a sigh of contentment. "I'd be happy to take some of the overflow off your hands. Thank you." Gabriel couldn't remember the last time he'd had homemade cookies. Or homemade bread...he didn't think he'd ever had that. His mouth was already watering.

Before their food came, his phone rang again. He checked the number and looked up. "I'm sorry, but I really need to take this."

She nodded and he headed out to answer—or evade answering—more questions.

When he got back to the table, the question that always came in the early stages of dating was asked. "So tell me about your family, Gabe," Breena asked as they tucked into the artfully presented plates of food in front of them.

Typically, he would avoid it or say he didn't have any family. But tonight, maybe because he was tired from a long day, he decided to share the truth. At least some of it. "Well, it's just me and my younger sister." At her questioning brow, he continued. "My parents were killed in a car accident when I was twenty-two. I was still in college, but I became my sister's sole provider and guardian."

"I'm really sorry, Gabe." Breena put her hand over his. "That must have been really hard for you and her."

He picked up his wine glass to give himself a minute. Usually, when Breena touched him, he felt sparks all up his arms. This time, however, he felt warmth spread from her hand to his heart. People often didn't know what to say when he told them his parents had died. It made them uncomfortable.

But Breena didn't look uncomfortable, just sad and compassionate.

"She was in the hospital for a long time and needed lots of care. Man, I hate hospitals. The sounds and smells…it's still hard to be around all that. I wound up having to quit college and got a job to take care of her. Thankfully, our parents had life insurance and health insurance, so the bulk of the initial costs were handled. But Carly needs constant care. I was able to get her into a rehab facility that did a good job helping her. When I moved to Nashville with Laci, I busted my butt so I could move Carly here as soon as possible."

"Is she here in Nashville?"

"She is." He smiled. It was impossible not to smile when he thought of Carly. She was the inspiration for everything he did. "We're close. I'm fortunate I get to see her often."

Breena smiled. "That's really nice. It's impressive your parents' death didn't break up the family. Good for you for being intentional in keeping it together."

If only she knew. He was no hero. He did what he had to do, but it never felt like enough.

"So what about you? Tell me about your family." He was ready to shift the focus off himself.

But before she was able to share anything, his phone rang. Again.

He checked the number and excused himself. Yet again. This one was one of the tour investors, wanting to be reassured the tour was still going to happen and Laci wasn't a bad risk for their money. Frustrated, he walked back in and stopped for a minute to look at Breena.

The waiter was back, talking with Breena when he returned. She didn't look mad or ticked off at him for having to take the calls, which surprised him. This was one reason he rarely had more than one or two dates with any woman. He settled back into his chair.

"I'm sorry about all the phone calls. I should have realized tonight would be a bad night to go out. Everyone is worried or wondering about Laci and the tour."

"Of course you have to deal with that," she said.

Again, he was struck that she wasn't mad or frustrated with him. Probably because this was a fake date, so her expectations were different. She *didn't* expect anything from him. He wasn't sure why the thought saddened him.

"You were about to tell me about your family," he reminded her.

"Well, Grace is pretty much it." She took a deep breath. "My mother left when I was in fourth grade, and that was the last I saw of her. Grace's mother had investigators track down both my mother and my father. I haven't done anything with the paperwork for my mother yet, but I've been in touch with the man who might be my father."

"Oh wow. How's that conversation going?" He couldn't imagine having to track down his parents. Of course, he couldn't imagine them leaving by choice. His parents had been great. They didn't have a lot of money, but they'd had an abundance of love.

She shrugged. "I always thought my father was some slacker who chose not to be involved in my life. It never occurred to me he might not even know I'm alive. The conversation is going slow, but I'm hoping he'll want to do a DNA test. And then we will know."

"And your mother?"

"She made her choice a long time ago. Honestly, and I feel bad thinking this, but I feel like my life probably turned out better because she left. Of course I didn't want her to go. My nine-year-old self loved her and wanted to be with her, even though life with my mom was chaotic. I was so fortunate Grace's family took me in. They became my foster family until I graduated from high school. Even after the foster system was done with me, they were my family. I like to think my mother knew I would be in good hands and would have a good life versus her just being a selfish woman."

"It sounds like the best possible outcome for your situation. No wonder you and Grace seem like sisters." He took a drink from his wineglass. "You know, there are times life deals us a really crappy hand. Sometimes, we're fortunate and get miracles or really special people who help us out. And sometimes, it's a lot of hard work and sacrifice that gets us through."

She picked up her wine glass and tilted it toward him. "Amen to that."

After paying the exorbitant bill for their less-than-satisfying meal, they headed out the door. He helped Breena into her coat, and they started walking toward his car. His phone rang, and he, once again, excused himself to take the call. He walked several steps away so he could hear better.

After finishing the call, Gabriel looked around for Breena. He heard her before he saw her. He walked in the direction of her laughter and found her talking to Tim, one of the "players" from Saturday night. He noticed how close Tim stood and how he leaned into her. She laughed at something he said, then she took a step back. The whole scene frustrated Gabriel. He had no claim to Breena, but Tim didn't know that.

"Well, hey there, Tim. What are you up to tonight?" He joined their cozy group and put his arm loosely around Breena's shoulders.

She smiled up at him and leaned in a little. It was a simple, subtle move, but it warmed his heart.

"I noticed you ignoring your beautiful date and wanted to see if she'd like to upgrade to someone who will pay more attention to her." Tim laughed when he said it, as if it were a joke, but Gabriel knew he was serious.

"I appreciate your concern for my date. And since she's still here, I'm going to assume she turned you down." He got a lot of satisfaction from Tim's annoyed look. He turned to Breena. "You ready to go, sweetheart?"

She grinned up at him. "I am. Let's go." She looked over at Tim. "Bye, Tim."

With his arm still around her, they turned and headed to his car. "I'm sorry about all the calls tonight. And I'm sorry Tim used my absence to hit on you."

She shrugged. "Like I said before, I know how to handle his type."

Having seen how she handled Tim, Gabriel was beginning to believe it. He wondered now how she would treat him when their fake dating was over.

"Hey, how's my favorite sister?" Gabriel's heart was full when he visited his sister the next day. She was the essence of pure love, and he would do anything to protect her from the world. Not many people even knew he had a sister. He couldn't believe he'd already told Breena about her.

"Gabe!" Carly rushed over and gave him a big hug, then she cackled. "I'm your only sister."

"Well, you're still my favorite. I brought some hot tea and cookies and thought we'd have a bit of a tea party while we catch up with each other today." He pulled out a thermos of the hot apple cinnamon tea that was Carly's favorite and a few of the cookies Breena had given him.

"Mmm, these are delicious. Who made them for you?"

"What? You think I didn't make them?" Gabriel tried to act insulted but grinned because it was true. "A new friend of mine made them and offered me some, so I thought I'd share them with you today."

"Is this a *girl*friend? I would be so happy if you had a girlfriend," Carly said with a wistful smile.

"No, no. Just a friend. You know I don't have time for girlfriends."

"Well, I think you're wrong about that, and you should make time for girlfriends and love."

"I love you and will always make time for you."

"I still think you're wrong but thank you for sharing your cookies. And thank your friend for making them."

As they caught up, Gabriel told her about his week, fielding calls from the media and some of the crazy rumors going around. Carly knew Laci, since he and Laci had been friends for so long.

"But Laci's okay, right?"

He wanted to assure his sister Laci was okay without compromising Laci's safety. "She is. But she wants privacy right now, so she's not telling anyone where she's staying. That has led to a lot of crazy stories by the press that I keep having to deal with."

"You work too hard, Gabe. You *need* to take time off." She'd said this before. And she was right; he did work too hard.

"I have to work hard, Carly. I can't lose everything I've spent the last ten years building."

"Well, I still think you should be able to slow down or take a vacation."

To divert her attention, he told her about the crazy restaurant he'd gone to with Breena, how small the portions were, how expensive the bill was.

Carly laughed. "Why would you take her there? Why not take her to your favorite restaurant? The yummy Italian one."

Good question, he thought. He couldn't tell her they were fake dating and needed to be seen. But he would have preferred to take Breena to Amati's. The food would have been much better, and he wouldn't have gone home hungry

"That's a really good question." He laughed in response. "Maybe that's where we should go next time."

Chapter 11

BREENA

Dear Ms. O'Malley,

I would be happy to do whatever you would like to solve this mystery. I would like to caution you not to get your hopes up too high. My wife and I were never able to have children, and the blame for that lay with me. So as much as it would thrill me to have a daughter, I just don't see how it could be possible, even though the timing seems to line up.

Let me know our next steps.

Regretful,

Peter

B REENA PULLED INTO THE Happy Valley parking lot, looking forward to a fun visit with
CeeCee. She had her athletic shoes on so they could
take a walk, and a basket with colorful nail polish
in case she wanted colorful toenails to match her
fingers.

After checking in, Breena headed down the
hallway to CeeCee's room. Before she reached it,
she could hear her laughing, which made Breena
wonder if she already had a guest.

When she reached the doorway, she froze.

Sitting with CeeCee was...Gabe.

So many questions flooded Breena's brain. What
was he doing there? Why was he visiting CeeCee? She
watched as he held her hand and listened to her stories.

This was a completely different Gabe she was glimpsing.

"Carly, you have purple fingernails. Where did you get *purple* fingernails?"

"My friend Bee helped me paint them. Aren't they great?"

"They're beautiful. Just as colorful as you are." Gabe gave her a big grin.

Breena's heart melted at how sweet Gabe was to CeeCee.

"Bee!" CeeCee noticed Breena in the doorway, then jumped up and rushed over to hug her. "My brother is here."

Breena was sure her jaw must have dropped. At the same moment, Gabe turned around and noticed her, his face draining of color.

"What are you doing here?" they said at the same time, his voice sounding angry and hers curious.

CeeCee took Breena's hand and led her into the room. "Bee, this is my brother, Gabe."

They just stared at each other.

CeeCee kept looking between Gabe and Breena, her pretty face scrunched-up with worry. She took Gabe's hand. "Gabe, this is Bee. I told you about her. She made my fingernails so pretty."

Gabe's sister, Carly, was CeeCee.

Breena's brain was working overtime, fitting all the pieces together. She didn't understand the anger she'd seen flit across his face. Why would he be angry about her visiting his sister? She'd mentioned her volunteer work to him. Well, she wasn't going to say anything and upset CeeCee.

"So is this the brother you told me about. The one you think should be my boyfriend?" she said with a grin on her face. She enjoyed watching Gabe's expression go from confused to startled. "Gabe, I didn't mean to interrupt your visit with your sister. I can come back at a different time." Breena headed toward the doorway.

"No, no. Don't go." He caught her arm before she could take more than a step. "I was just heading out anyway. Carly, would you like Breena to stay with you for a little while?" Breena's heart almost broke at the love for his sister that showed on his face.

"Yes. Can you stay, Bee?" CeeCee looked so hopeful, she couldn't say no.

"I would love to, CeeCee."

Gabe leaned down to hug his sister and kiss her cheek. "I love you, Goof. Have fun with Breena."

"See you later, alligator." She said with a grin.

"Gotta go, buffalo." Gabe said. Every time he left, he tried to come up with a new way to say bye to her. It was a game they'd started about a year ago.

Carly giggled at his response. "Love you, Gabe."

As soon as Gabe was gone, Breena leaned in conspiratorially. "You were right, CeeCee. He *is* tall, dark, and handsome." Breena waggled her eyebrows, making CeeCee laugh.

Breena offered to go for a walk with CeeCee. "Should I call you CeeCee or Carly?" she asked as they walked along the paths outside.

CeeCee snickered. "I like CeeCee, but Gabe will only call me Carly."

"Well, okay. I'll call you CeeCee." Breena grinned.

"How do you know my brother?"

Breena wasn't sure how much she should say, so she kept it simple. "A friend of mine introduced us."

"Is he your boyfriend?" CeeCee asked with a sly smile.

Breena laughed. "No, just a friend."

"Wait." CeeCee's eyes went wide. "Are you the friend who made the cookies?"

"The chocolate chunk cookies?"

CeeCee nodded.

"I did make those. How did you know? You're one smart cookie, CeeCee."

CeeCee giggled. "Gabe brought tea and cookies today, and we had a tea party. Your cookies were yummy."

"Aw, thanks." She gave CeeCee a little hug, ignoring what the mental image of Gabe having a tea party with his sister was doing to her heart. "I'll bring you cookies any time you want."

CeeCee's eyes went wide. "Any time? Wow."

"I'm happy to make them for you."

A couple of hours later, back at the penthouse, Breena was sitting in the living room with Laci and Grace, enjoying a cup of coffee and cookies. "I met Gabe's sister today."

Laci's eyes went wide. "He introduced you to Carly?"

"Gabe has a sister?" Grace asked at the same time.

"Well, it was sort of an accidental meeting." Breena grinned. "Apparently, the CeeCee I've been visiting is Carly, his sister. Gabe was finishing up his visit with her when I got there."

"How'd he take that? He's very protective of her," Laci said.

Breena shrugged. "At dinner last night, he mentioned he had a sister, but I didn't connect it was CeeCee. And when we first saw each other today, I could have sworn he was angry I was there."

"Wait, he *told* you he had a sister?" Laci looked surprised. "I don't think he's ever told a date he has a sister."

"Well, it's not like they're really dating, Laci," Grace said.

Breena frowned a little at the comment, but it was true. She didn't know what to think about what Laci said. Gabe was such a contradiction. He was a self-proclaimed workaholic but regularly made time to see his sister. He didn't want a girlfriend or love but acted jealous when Tim was talking to her last night. Seeing him with his sister today had completely thrown her heart into overdrive. He was very open with his love and affection for her.

She shook her head. "Gabe is very confusing."

Laci laughed. "That he is. He's had some hard things happen in his life, and they've changed him. I think he's afraid to love, to feel the pain of someone leaving again."

Breena nodded. "He told me about their parents getting killed in an accident. I can't imagine how hard that must have been for him. And then to assume responsibility for Carly so young."

"He was devastated when they died. And when Carly wound up with a brain injury...well, he grew up awfully quick that summer. He had to."

"Oh, how horrible." Grace's eyes teared up.

"I told Gabe about my family last night too. How my mother left when I was nine." She took a deep breath, and Grace reached over to cover her hand. She smiled at her friend. "I was so fortunate when Grace's parents took me in and treated me like a daughter. They became my foster family. Even when I was no longer in the system, they still kept me. If it hadn't been for Grace's family, my childhood would have looked very different."

"Your mother left you? Why?" Laci looked stunned. "Sorry, none of my business."

"No, it's okay. She left because of a guy. He was very possessive and didn't like having a kid in the picture. She left so I wouldn't be in their picture anymore. Love can really mess people up."

"I'm pretty sure what your mother and that guy had wasn't love, Bree. You know that, right?" Grace said.

Breena nodded but wasn't sure she believed it. "Yeah, but she said she loved me. And she left me." She sat looking down at her hands for a few minutes. "For a while, I pretended like Grace and her parents were my real family, not just my foster family. It seemed easier than dealing with the feelings connected to my mother. I didn't want to think about the fact that she chose some loser guy over her own daughter. That she could so easily leave me."

Grace leaned over and wrapped her in a side hug, then headed to the kitchen for more cookies.

"And you never heard from her after she left?" Laci asked.

"No. But Grace's parents had investigators track down my parents, both of them. I just got the paperwork from the lawyer last week." Breena twisted her hands in her lap. "I've actually been emailing the man who might be my father."

Grace froze on her way back to the table. "What?"

"Oh my gosh, wow. So you never knew your father?" Laci asked.

Breena looked at Grace. "It's been so crazy lately...and I really don't know if he's my father or not, so I just didn't mention it. Sorry."

"No, it's okay. I'm just surprised. Tell us all about it," Grace said.

Breena shared about the emails that had been going back and forth between Peter and her. "Anyway, he seems like a decent person. He was genuinely shocked to hear he might have a daughter. Just this morning he agreed to do a DNA test."

"Wow. And how are you feeling about all of this?" Grace asked.

"Well, if he *is* my father, it's weird to learn he didn't reject me, and instead didn't even know about me. Like I said, he seems like a nice guy. I have no idea if he'll want any kind of relationship with me or not. It's a lot to ask of someone." Breena looked down at her hands, unsure what to say next.

"Did you look at your mother's paperwork?" Grace asked.

"No. I want to, but at the same time, I don't want to. Loving her and her leaving crushed me. It messed me up in so many ways. All my relationships with men are based on her. I hate that."

"You were nine," Laci said. "You dealt with it like a nine-year-old, but don't let her dictate what you think about love. She sounds like a bad example to follow, don't you think? Not that I'm one to be giving advice on love, mind you."

Laci was right. Why was she setting her love standard by her mom? She gave Laci a small smile. "Why does life and love have to be so complicated?"

"If you want to read your mother's information now, we can be here for you," Grace said tentatively.

Breena's eyes went wide.

Laci moved to sit on her other side. "Of course we'll be here for you."

Breena took a deep breath. "If you're sure. Hang on a sec." She ran through the dining room to her bedroom and picked up the envelope from her bedside table.

She came back to the living room and set the envelope on the coffee table. The name Maeve Erin O'Malley stared at them.

Grace reached over and took her hand. "You want to open it, or would you like me to?"

Breena stared straight ahead, at the envelope. "Do you mind?"

So Grace picked up the envelope and ran her finger under the flap to open it. She unfolded the papers tucked inside.

"It looks like it's a timeline from after she left Florida. Do you want to hear it?"

Breena shook her head. "No, just skip to the end." She held Laci's hand and stared down at her lap. Did she really want to know where her mother was?

She could hear Grace flipping through the papers and then gently try to straighten out the folds to read it.

Grace gasped softly, then started reading aloud. "'November 13, 2017. We traced Ms. O'Malley to the outskirts of Nashville, Tennessee. On November 13, she was admitted to Nashville General Hospital with a gash under her right eye, a broken nose, and two cracked ribs. The doctors treated her, and she was released the next day to the boyfriend.'"

Laci's hand tightened on Breena's.

"'November 15, 2017. Ms. O'Malley was admitted again to the hospital with serious injuries. Her left arm was broken, another rib broken, and she had several lacerations in her left leg. She checked out of the hospital the next morning.'"

"My goodness," Laci commented, "I hope she didn't go back to that boyfriend."

Breena wasn't sure what to say or think. This was her mother after all. But she was the mother who abandoned her.

Grace continued reading. "'We found a gravesite at Nashville Memorial Cemetery for Maeve Erin O'Malley. The dates on the headstone read January 3, 1970 to November 18, 2017.'"

Breena sat, quietly absorbing the information she'd heard. Her mother was dead and buried in Nashville. Of all places, her mother wound up here, in Nashville, in the end.

"There's another paper here in the envelope," Grace said quietly. She held it up for Breena to see. "Shall I read it?"

Breena nodded, tears running down her cheeks. Laci handed her a tissue, then held her hand again.

"Oh my gosh," Grace gasped. "It's from Mama."

Breena turned to look at Grace, her wide eyes matching Grace's. "What?" Breena's heart hammered in her chest. What could Marilyn possibly have to do with this?

"'Darling Breena,'" Grace read aloud. "'If you are reading this, that means you want to know what happened to your mother. I was sworn to secrecy at the time of these events but was told if you ever wanted to know what happened to your mother, I could share this with you.

"'Your mother was brought to my secret apartment late one night in November 2017. She was in bad shape, and I wasn't sure why she came to me instead of staying in the hospital. But God works in mysterious ways, and apparently, he wanted me to be part of the end of this woman's journey.

"'When she was first brought in, I didn't even realize who she was. I'd forgotten how young she was. But then I read through her paperwork and knew without a doubt she was the same Maeve who had blessed our family with you.

"'When she realized who I was, she wanted to talk. Well, that's not accurate. She wanted to listen. She wanted to hear all about you and how your life has gone. She was so happy to hear you graduated high school in the top ten percent. That you went to nursing school and traveled around the country helping others. She was very proud of what you'd made of your life.

"'She asked me to tell you how very sorry she was for the choices she made, but she made them trying to think of you first. She knew you'd have a better life with us—at least she hoped you would—and she needed to leave you free to grow and blossom. She asked me to tell you she always loved you.

"'She was only with me for three days before she passed away. The damage done to her and the damage she'd done to her body by her lifestyle had caught up to her. She died in peace, knowing you are happy and healthy, hoping one day you can find the heart to forgive her.

"'I love you, darling girl, Marilyn.'"

They sat in silence for a full minute before Grace and Laci both reached over and enveloped Breena in a hug. When they finally pulled apart, their faces were wet from tears. Laci handed out tissues, and they contemplated what they'd heard.

"Wow." Grace spoke first. "I can't believe my mom was with yours at the end. How're you doing?"

Breena shrugged and wiped her nose. "I'm not sure. This is a lot to take in. Mom was only forty-seven when she died. That's so young. I really want to be mad at her, but I can't get past being sad. What a sad way for her life to end."

Grace nodded and rubbed her back. "Can I get you anything?"

"No, I think I'm going to lay down for a bit. I just need a good cry. Thank you both for being here with me for this." She stood and hugged them both before heading to her bedroom

Dear Mr. Simmonds,

I appreciate your willingness to explore this with me. I've attached the information on how and where to get the test. I've already submitted mine, so we'll get the results at the same time.

I know this isn't what you were expecting when you opened that first email from me, but I'm glad you opened it and responded, regardless of what the results are.

Grateful,

Breena

Chapter 12

GABRIEL

GABRIEL STOOD IN THE lobby of The Athenian with Jillian as they waited for Brian to
buzz up to the penthouse.

"Sorry to bother you, Miss Parson. I have Officer Jillian and Mr. van Neugh here. May I send
them up?" Brian asked.

A minute or so later, the elevator doors opened,
and Jillian and Gabriel walked into the apartment,
both with serious expressions.

"Hi, guys, what's up?" Grace stood from the
couch to greet them. Laci was sitting next to her..
Gabriel briefly wondered where Breena was.

"I've got some official business to talk to Laci
about." Jillian walked into the living room and sat
down in a chair by the couch.

Just then, Breena walked into the room and headed to the couch to sit on the other side of Laci. Gabriel noticed her nose was red and her eyes looked flat. Sad, maybe.

"Laci," Jillian started, "I wanted to let you know before you heard it elsewhere, Hank tried to break into your property today. We caught him trying to silence the alarm after he'd broken a window."

Laci's eyes were wide with fear, her face pale. She opened her mouth, but nothing came out. Breena and Grace held her hands, offering support.

Jillian continued. "He's in jail. Without bail, so he'll be there until his trial. He's added a whole list of charges to his record today, including assaulting an officer, breaking and entering, and trespassing. He won't go anywhere anytime soon."

"So..."

Gabriel knelt in front of her, his hands on her knees. "He's behind bars, Lace. It's safe now. I've already got someone getting the window boarded up for tonight. It'll be replaced tomorrow. I'm guessing you can go home anytime you want."

Laci's eyes went wide again, and he could feel her legs trembling beneath his hands.

"I think it would be good if she stayed here another couple of days," Breena said. "I'd like to keep an eye on those ribs for a little bit longer before I clear her. If that's okay with you, Laci?"

He could see the relief on Laci's face.

"Oh...well, I guess I could stay a little longer," Laci said.

Gabriel had seen the frightened look on Laci's face when he said she could go home. He was surprised but pleased when Breena jumped in with the answer—to give Laci a few more days here instead of having to go home by herself. Granted, he wasn't in healthcare, but he would bet Laci was fine, physically, to be home by herself. That Breena would be generous with her time and space shouldn't have surprised him.

Jillian took off after sharing her information, but Gabriel decided to stick around for a bit.

"So how did Hank get caught?" Laci asked.

"I got a call from a reporter, of all people. One I've done a few favors for. He called and said he was hanging out at your house, waiting to see if you'd show up today. Instead, he saw Hank drive up. Hank parked down the road a bit—trying to hide his car, I guess. He watched him climb the fence, then called me."

Gabriel watched all three women's mouths fall open, his eyes lingering on Breena's lips a little too long. He shook his head to clear it.

"So I headed over to your house and called Jillian on my way. I parked in front of Hank's car and had the reporter park behind him, blocking him in case he tried to leave before Jillian arrived. But Jillian and Mike got there just after me. I opened the gates, we drove up to the house, and they caught Hank coming out the kitchen door. Randy, the reporter, got an exclusive out of the deal, and Hank got a one-way trip to jail."

"Did he take anything?" Laci's voice was strong, even though her hands were clutched tightly in her lap.

"He had a couple of your awards and some artwork. Guess he was hoping for some quick cash. The police took the items for evidence, but you'll get them back," he assured her.

Grace spoke up for the first time. "Laci, you're welcome to stay here as long as you want to. Even without a medical excuse. Breena and I enjoy your company, so it's not a problem."

Breena nodded. "And Gabe, since Laci doesn't have to be in hiding anymore, you don't have to 'date' me. I'm sure it's inconvenient having to take me to events."

He frowned a little. Why would she think it was inconvenient to date her?

"We could continue dating...if you think it's necessary?" He asked the question of Laci.

"I think it makes sense for you two to continue fake dating as long as I stay here," Laci said with a grin.

He nodded and looked at Breena. Something was still off with her, but he wasn't sure what. "Speaking of, I have a dinner I need to go to this weekend. Would you like to join me?"

He watched Breena look at Laci, then back to him. He wasn't sure what the look was that passed between them. "Sure. I can go. What's the occasion?"

"It's a formal dinner, black-tie affair. I honestly can't remember what the occasion is at the moment. But I'll figure it out before I pick you up."

"Sure, no problem. Saturday night?"

"Yep. I'll pick you up at six."

The next morning, Gabriel listened to tapes of several new artists who were trying to make it here in Nashville. He liked having a variety of entertainers to manage, and he wanted a few new artists to round out his clientele. He listened again to the tapes Ms. Starr had given him and decided to set up an audition day for his five favorites. He wanted Laci to be part of the process, since they would be on tour with her. He wasn't sure, though, how that could happen. Maybe she could listen from behind a panel or glass or something. He'd have to figure it out.

Kelly tapped on his office door. "Excuse me, sir." She waited until he looked up. "Two things. One, the new window is installed at Laci's house. The contractor just called to let us know. And two, there's a Miss O'Malley here to see you."

Gabe was smiling before he could catch himself.

"Shall I send her in, sir?"

"Thank you, Kelly. And yes, please send her in." Gabriel ran his fingers through his hair, trying to tame it. He stood behind his desk, then felt like that was too formal so sat back down. Breena had never visited him at his office. His brain went into overdrive trying to figure out why she'd be here.

But as soon as he saw her in the doorway, he found he didn't care why she'd come. She was took her coat and hat off, then shook out her hair, which caught the light spilling in from the window and seemed to sparkle.

"Not going to say hello?" She smiled at him, her eyes dancing with humor.

He jumped up. "Sorry. You just looked so lovely standing there." He could see her confusion at the compliment. "Hello there." He walked over and took her coat and hat. Kelly smiled as he closed the door.

"What a pleasant surprise," he said, meaning it.

"Thanks. I have a quick question." She paused, and at his nod, continued, "Laci would like to get a few things from her house without drawing media attention. I have an idea but wanted to run it by you."

"Sure, what're you thinking?" He was curious about what they'd come up with.

"Well, we have a lot of disguises and props in the secret apartment and thought we could disguise her. Maybe a dark wig. A little padding to give her a different shape. Different clothes, of course. But what would be the reason for going to her house?"

"I like the disguise idea." With his chin resting on his right hand he looked at the ceiling, thinking. "I've been trying to figure out something along these lines too. I have several bands I want to audition, but I need Laci to hear them too. I wonder if we could combine these tasks. I can set the band auditions at the studio behind her house. She comes early in disguise, as a band member maybe, gets her things together, then comes to the studio and listens to the bands."

Breena thought about it. "That could work. When were you thinking?"

"I could probably set something up in the next couple of days." He walked around and sat behind his desk, looking at his computer. "Okay, today is Thursday. I'll try to get it organized for tomorrow afternoon or Saturday morning."

"Perfect. What are the bands auditioning for?"

"Well, two things, though they won't know that. I'm looking for some new clients to represent, and we need some fresh opening acts for Laci's world tour."

"Oh, interesting. Am I allowed to sit in and listen?" She grinned.

"Of course. I'll be interested to see what you think of them." It gave him a thrill that she wanted to be part of his world for a bit. He stood as she prepared to leave. "You look better today," he said without meaning to.

"Better? Than what?" Her eyebrows furrowed in question.

"Yesterday when Jillian and I came by, you looked...sad, I guess."

She nodded but didn't respond. "You should have Jillian and Grace join us. They're both musical. Me, I just enjoy listening."

"Really? Grace and Jillian have musical talent?" Gabe was intrigued.

"Well, Jilly has some mad karaoke skills. She has a great voice. Grace plays piano, and she played some sort of horn in the marching band in high school and college."

"Huh, who knew?" He stepped closer, grinning at her. "You sure you don't have some musical talents hidden in there?"

Breena stood inches from him. He could feel her breath on his face.

"My talents aren't musical." She winked and walked out.

He let out a deep breath and headed back to his desk, knowing it would be a while before he got that thought out of his head.

Chapter 13

BREENA

Dear Breena,

Mission accomplished.

I'm not sure what happens next, but I assume we sit and wait. This reminds me of when Cindy and I were trying to get pregnant, always waiting to see if that little stick would say "pregnant" or not.

I'm nervous. And hopeful.

Your potential father,

Peter

ON THE WAY BACK to the penthouse, Breena did something she hadn't planned to do. She decided to swing by the Nashville Memorial Cemetery and look for her mom.

She thought it was interesting that Gabe noticed she was feeling off yesterday. She had to have looked a mess when he stopped by. Red nose and puffy eyes from crying. Her hair probably all over the place from lying down.

She followed the GPS directions to the small cemetery and parked her car. Hopefully, she'd be able to find her mom's marker without too much trouble. It was a beautiful and peaceful spot, and she wondered if Marilyn had chosen it.

Since she had no idea where to look, she started at the first row and decided to be methodical about it—just go down each row, one at a time. Eventually, she should find the right headstone. She wished she had a little more information to work with. All she knew was that her mom had been buried here in 2017, so she should be able to discard the really old headstones.

She wandered down one row after another, reading the names as they went by. She was finally rewarded for her efforts in the fifth row, about halfway down. There was a light gray headstone with a small angel on top.

Maeve Erin O'Malley

January 3, 1970 – November 18, 2017

Remembered with love

for the hard choices you made.

Now she knew Grace's mother had been involved. She sat on the ground in front of the grave and stared at the angel.

"Mom, I know you want forgiveness, but I'm not sure I can do that. I know you did what you thought was best. And I have a good life. But I grew up thinking I had two parents who didn't love me."

She sat quietly for a moment and wiped tears from her cheek.

"And now, I find out you did love me. You left *because* you loved me. And my father..." She blew out a noisy breath. "I wish you had told me about him."

Breena looked at the rows of headstones surrounding Maeve's, then turned back..

"When I was confused and didn't know what to do, you always asked me what I knew for sure. So right now, what I know for sure is that for several years when

I was young, I had a mom who loved me. After you left, I had Grace's family who loved me. And at the moment, I may have found the father I never knew. But maybe, once again, I'll have a parent who loves me."

She pulled her jacket tighter around her chest. It was getting chilly.

"I guess when I look at it like that, I've been surrounded by love my whole life. Maybe I will be able to forgive you someday. I'll let you know."

Breena stood up and wiped her pants off before heading back to her car.

Later that evening, Gabe called her to say he'd set up the auditions for four of the five bands. He would meet them at Laci's house at ten the next morning.

"I'll unlock the gate and let you in, so it looks like you're musicians. Looking forward to seeing what disguises you come up with."

"Sounds good. We'll see you in the morning."

"Well..." She turned to Laci after hanging up. "It looks like you're about to have your debut outing tomorrow morning. Ready to audition for the awesome Laci Love?"

Laci laughed. "I don't know. She's pretty amazing."

"How're you feeling about going out in public? It's been a bit."

"Yeah, it's weird to be nervous. I'm used to the media and fans."

"True, but your sense of safety has been breached. It's going to take some time to build it back up, I think."

"You're right. Going back to my house feels...scary, I guess. I hate that Hank took my sense of security from me." Laci frowned.

"You'll get it back. Give yourself time." Breena grabbed her hand. "Let's go find us some disguises to wear."

Breena was excited she and Laci would be going out the next morning and hoped they didn't attract any attention from the media. She looked at Laci and noted the nerves in her expression.

"Just so you know, Laci, you're welcome to stay as long as you want. Please don't feel like you have to leave just because someone else says you should."

Laci stopped in the closet in Breena's bedroom and turned to look at her. "Thank you, Breena. You are one of the kindest, most genuine people I have ever met. You get a little jaded when you've been in this industry as long as I have. I think I'd like to stay here with you for a bit longer. Honestly, I'm not sure I ever want to live in that house again." She shivered a little.

They continued through to the hidden apartment and back to the bedroom.

"You know, I haven't had a break in at least ten years. And girlfriends...I can't tell you how long it's been since I've had a female friend. One who didn't want something from me. I hope you don't mind I count you as a friend."

Breena blinked back some tears and hugged Laci. "I'm honored to call you friend."

Laci looked around the room. "Alrighty then. Let's get dolled up."

Breena pulled all of the wigs from the closet. Laci tucked her long honey-blonde hair in a net while Breena did the same with her own hair. Then they went to town, trying on all the different wigs. Long blonde hair. Short blonde bob. Short brown pixie cut. Sleek black with bangs. They laughed about how the wavy red wig looked very similar to Breena's hair.

"Okay, I think this is my favorite." Laci was wearing the brown pixie-cut wig. "I like this cut on me. I may have to get a wig like this for the tour. Gabe would probably have a cow if I cut my hair. You know, I have an image to maintain." She rolled her eyes, then looked at Breena, who had the black wig on. "Ugh, no. Too dark for your skin tone. Go back to the blonde bob. That was really cute on you."

"Okay, now for our costumes." Breena put the extra wigs back in the closet and started pulling out some clothes in their sizes.

"Ooh, this is perfect for you." Laci held up a tiny black leather miniskirt.

"Um, where's the rest of it?" she laughed.

"Can I choose your outfit? Please. I have this image in my head that would look so good on you."

Breena couldn't help but go along with her enthusiasm. Laci picked out an outfit Breena would never have chosen for herself, matching the black skirt with a black leather bustier that laced up the front, a pair of fishnet stockings, black cowboy boots, and a black cowboy hat.

"Dang, girl. You look hot!"

Breena laughed. "I do, don't I."

"Gabe's going to swallow his tongue." Laci laughed.

"Oh, he won't even notice." Breena could feel her face getting warm—she hated that she blushed so easily—but she secretly hoped Gabe would notice her.

"Oh girl, he's not dead. He'll notice. Besides, I've seen the way he looks at you."

Breena didn't want to ask, but the words came out on their own. "How does he look at me?"

"Like he wants to eat you up."

She couldn't think of anything to say out loud, but her brain was swirling. When she'd first met Gabe she thought he'd be fun for a fling, but now that she knew him better, she wanted more. More than he was able to give and more than she knew what to do with.

She cleared her throat and shifted the attention to Laci. "Okay, my turn to pick your outfit."

As she rifled through the closet, looking for clothes for Laci, she wondered what Gabe's reaction would be when he saw her. She pulled out a pair of red leather shorty-shorts; they would match her black leather vibe. "Hmm, I like these." She held the shorts up for Laci to see. "I don't see a good top to go with them though."

Laci joined her in the closet, and they rummaged through everything. She found a bright red bra, and Breena matched it with a sheer black long-sleeved top. The red cowboy boots they found finished off the look.

Outfits on, they checked themselves out in the large mirror.

"We look good," Laci said.

"Right? We need to be a girl band. We'd kill it." Breena laughed. "Except for the fact that I can't sing."

"Hmm, you can be the tambourine girl." Laci laughed. She looked around the room, at the clothes strewn across the bed. "Man, I haven't had this much fun in a long time."

Just then, the buzzer in Breena's apartment rang. Laci's head shot up.

"Shoot. Hang on a sec. Let me see who's here." Breena ran across to the other apartment, pulling down her skimpy black skirt, and answered the call.

The elevator door opened, and Jillian walked in.

"Love what you've done to yourself." She gave Breena a sassy grin. "Where's the party?"

Breena laughed. "Laci and I are going to her house tomorrow. She has to pick up some things so she can stay here longer, and she'll listen to some bands audition to go on tour with her. But we're going in disguise as a band."

"Ooh, I'm off tomorrow. Can I come? I want to be in your band."

"You know it's just for show, right?" Laci said, walking in.

"I do, but I'd still love to join you. I love listening to bands."

"Well, come on back, and let's see if there's any more leather in that magical closet." Laci laughed.

Breena followed them through the secret panel to the "magical" closet, ready to doll up Jillian. She had to agree with Laci; she hadn't had this much fun in years. She was looking forward to the next morning. A lot.

Dear Peter,

My fingers are crossed!

I feel like I should tell you, I found my mom. Unfortunately, she passed away a few years ago. I was able to visit her grave today and had a little heart-to-heart with her. She wants me to forgive her for leaving me, but I'm just not sure whether I can do that or not.

I now know she left to try to give me a better life—and I did have a good life. I also now know she loved me. I'll be honest, that came as a shock. I thought when she left, she never thought about me again. But that wasn't the case.

Anyway, I'm waiting in hope,

Breena

Chapter 14

GABRIEL

GABRIEL FELT LIKE HIS brain had exploded. He was looking at Breena...except she was a blonde-haired vixen in an incredible black leather outfit. Her skirt was very short and molded to her hips like it was made for her. But the vest-looking thing she wore as a top—it was the sexiest thing he'd ever seen. Her creamy white skin and lovely cleavage were on display, doing things to his brain.

Holy moly, he was in trouble.

While he already knew Breena was a beautiful woman, this was a level of sexy he hadn't been prepared for. He shook his head, trying to get those synapses snapping again.

"So...wow!" Swallowing hard, trying to breathe past the lump in his throat, he walked up to her. Crowded her. He wasn't able to *not* be close. "You,

Breena O'Malley, are a vision. An incredibly sexy vision." His voice was husky. He touched the ends of her blonde wig. "I like the blonde."

He could feel her breath on his face. He leaned down, millimeters from the lips that had been tempting him for days.

"Ahem." Laci and Jillian got out of the car.

He jerked back and noticed a look pass between them. He took a small step back from Breena and looked at the other two women. "You ladies look like you're in a girl band. Do all women have leather outfits just hanging around in their closets?"

"You should have seen the outfits we rejected." Laci laughed. Her red leather showcased her slender body.

"Jillian, nice to see you. Did y'all run out of leather?"

Jillian laughed. "Actually, yes." She looked at her low-rise jean-shorts paired with fishnet stockings and a turquoise bralette, Grace's turquoise cowboy boots, and her own black leather jacket.

"Now put your eyeballs back in your head and let us into the house. It's freezing out here, and as you can see, we're not wearing much," Laci said.

"Right." It took a moment to remember what he was doing. Then he looked closer at Laci. "Tell me that's a wig?"

"Of course it's a wig. But I really like it. I might do something like this one day." She ran her fingers through the wig's short pixie cut.

"Well, it looks great. Not at all like Laci Love, which I suppose is the point. Come on in," he said, unlocking the front door.

Once inside, Gabriel went to the studio while the three women headed up to Laci's bedroom. After checking the equipment in the studio, he made some coffee in the kitchen to bring into the lounge outside the studio.

Within half an hour, the four bands had all arrived and brought their instruments inside. He explained that he'd like each band to play a few songs. The first band piled into the studio; they were three young men who'd been eyeing Laci, Breena, and Jillian. Not that Gabriel blamed them.

Laci sat next to him as they listened to the music. "I remember this band from the tapes," she said softly. She closed her eyes and hummed along.

The next artist was a solo man, Jasper Lane. He wore Wranglers and a shirt with pearl snaps. Gabriel looked at Laci, trying to get a read on what she thought.

"He's good," she commented.

After listening to the last band, Gabriel was about to wrap up the morning. The young man who had gone second, Jasper, stood up.

"Wait a minute." He looked at Laci. "These ladies haven't gone. Don't they have to audition? Or are they getting by on their looks?"

Gabriel looked at the man. "I've already heard them."

Laci stood up. "You know what? I'm happy to play for this gentleman," she said, looking at him. "Come on, ladies."

Gabriel noticed Breena's eyes go wide as she started whispering furiously to Laci, but Laci just nodded as they walked into the studio. When they were ready, Laci had one of her guitars and Jillian sat on a stool next while Breena stood in the background with a bongo drum. Gabriel smiled at that. Clever move, he thought. But he was curious about Jillian at the mic. Breena had said she could sing. Now he'd find out if she was right.

Laci started playing the guitar, one of her older songs, then started singing.

Gabriel heard Jasper grumbling behind him. "Oh brother, they're singing one of Laci Love's songs. She doesn't even *sound* like her."

Jillian came in on the chorus with harmonies. They sounded good together. Really good. This was a day of surprises. Breena had mentioned Jillian liked to sing, but she had real skill.

The other musicians all stood up, listening to Laci and Jillian, smiling. Except, of course, Jasper. He stood in the background, frowning. Gabriel didn't pay attention to him though. He was watching Breena on the drum. She was standing behind the large drum to the right of Laci. Her rhythm was good, even if her volume wasn't.

As the song came to an end, Gabriel thanked them and waited until they came out of the studio before addressing the group.

"Thank you all for coming today on such short notice. I enjoyed listening to you, and we'll be making a decision soon as to who will join Laci on her world tour."

Jasper, the grumbler, spoke up again. "You mean *you* are going to make the decision. Apparently, Laci couldn't make the time to join us today. Instead, we get Laci-wannabes." He looked at Laci, Jillian, and Breena, then around at the rest of the bands. "And these."

Gabriel looked at him. "Have you ever been on tour, Jasper?"

"No, why?"

"Well, typically when on tour, everyone is pretty much a big family. All the artists hang out together. Quite frankly, I'm not sure you'd fit in."

"What?" He looked taken back. "I'll get along fine...*with Laci.*"

Laci stepped forward. "Thank you for coming today, but I don't want you touring with us." She pulled her short wig off, and her long blonde hair came tumbling down.

Gabriel enjoyed watching the reaction on each of the faces, but especially Jasper's. His eyes went wide and his face grew pale.

"You are welcome to leave now."

Gabriel walked him to the front door. "A little advice?"

Jasper turned and looked at Gabriel.

"Don't be an ass when you're auditioning for the biggest opportunity to come your way. You've got a great voice, but you need to be able to work with others to make it in this town."

Jasper walked out the door without a word. Gabriel shook his head but knew it wasn't his problem to figure that guy out.

He headed back to the studio to hustle the others along and get them on their way so Laci could go back to Breena's. When he walked into the lounge, he saw Laci sitting with the other musicians asking questions. She enjoyed this part of being a musician, and he didn't want to deprive her of it. Especially since she'd been so closed off from the world for a week.

After several minutes, he stood up. "Okay, folks, thank you for coming by this afternoon. I appreciate you accommodating our schedule and enjoyed hearing you." He looked at Laci, who nodded. "I'll be in touch shortly with some news, and we'll go from there."

The other bands packed up, and Gabriel walked them to the front door. When he got back, Laci, Breena, and Jillian were coming down the stairs with suitcases. Laci grabbed her guitar, and they headed out.

Gabriel looked at Breena. "You mind if I come by? I'd like to talk this through with Laci while it's fresh."

Breena looked at Laci, then back at Gabe. "Sure. We'll see you there."

He grabbed a couple of big suitcases, locked the front door, and they all headed out.

Saturday evening after the elevator doors opened, Gabriel checked his tuxedo in the entryway mirror, straightening the green ribbon attached to his lapel. His dark hair was combed into submission tonight, and his jaw clean shaven. His eyes were drawn to the words written on the mirror, *Smile*, and he remembered what Breena had said to him on their first date—that he didn't smile enough. Catching sight of her by fireplace, he couldn't help but smile. Breena was lovely in a full-length, long-sleeved, low cut silver velvet dress. She looked stunning.

"I feel like I should have brought you flowers."

Breena smiled. "Well, I like tulips."

"I'll keep that in mind." He grinned at her. "You look beautiful. I like this outfit almost as much as the one yesterday." Gabriel walked to her.

"Ha! You won't be seeing that one again. I think it's the last you'll see of Leather and Laci." Breena laughed.

"Leather and Laci?" Gabriel arched an eyebrow. "Clever."

"We decided last night we needed a name for our band. Leather and Laci was the winner. We had an encore show here in the apartment after a couple glasses of wine, but the group is now officially in retirement."

Gabriel looked around. "Speaking of, where's Laci?"

"She's taking a nap. We stayed up kind of late last night, so she's catching up."

He was now standing right in front of her. "I'm sorry I missed your encore concert," he said in a low voice. "I'd really love to see that outfit again."

She laughed as he waggled his eyebrows. But dang if he didn't mean it. He really would love to see her in that outfit again.

"Did I mention you look gorgeous tonight?" He looked at her figure-hugging dress.

"You might have mentioned it."

Her shaky voice thrilled him. He ran the back of his fingers down her darkening cheeks, enjoying the softness of her skin. "Hmm, well. I guess it needed to be said again."

She took a quick, shaky breath and a small step back. "Guess it's probably time to go?"

"Sure." He smiled at her and helped her into her coat.

During the short ride to the hotel, they talked about the bands who had auditioned yesterday and the young, overly confident upstart Laci had shot down.

"I knew that guy was going to be an issue from the get-go. He had an arrogant energy about him. While we were listening to the other bands, he had a lot to say," Breena said.

"What do you mean?"

"Oh, he had all kinds of comments about everyone. What they were wearing. How they were singing. He definitely wasn't a team player."

"Hmm, glad he's not in the picture then. That kind of personality is hard on a tour. Maybe you should listen to the fifth band with me tomorrow. You seem good at reading people."

He saw her look over at him. "Sure. I'd enjoy that."

Gabriel paused and gathered his thoughts before asking the next question. "Do you think Laci's ever going to move back into her house?"

"I'm not sure. She was a little freaked out going in yesterday."

"And you're good with her at your place for now?"

"I am. For as long as she wants to stay. It's certainly big enough. And with Grace gone most days, working either on her wedding or Hope's House, it's nice to have Laci around."

They pulled up to the hotel entrance and the valet took the car, and Gabriel put his arm around Breena as they walked in. He'd supported Nashville Grey Love Foundation for the past five years, but this was the first time he'd actually used his tickets. He was happy to support this foundation that funded research into traumatic brain injuries like his sister's.

After checking their coats, they found their table and were pleased to see their companions included Tom and Gigi Marshall.

"Oh my goodness, Tom. Look who showed up this year." Mrs. Marshall smiled at Gabriel and Breena. "Breena, darling, it's lovely to see you again."

Gabriel laughed. "Hi, Mrs. Marshall, Tom. If I'd known I'd be sitting with you, I would have tried to make it all those years I missed."

"You don't normally come to this? But you said you bought tickets every year?" Breena looked confused.

Mrs. Marshall leaned over. "He buys tickets, then never shows up. What'd you have to do to get him here?"

Breena laughed. "I just said 'yes.'"

"Well, it's lovely to see you two here tonight. This is going to be fun."

Gabriel excused himself and went to the bar to grab drinks. He didn't usually enjoy this type of event, but he was happy to be here with Breena...happy they were sitting with the Marshalls. And from the looks of it, there might be dancing later in the evening. He'd have to get Breena on the dance floor. He wanted her in his arms for a slow song.

"Well, hey there, Gabriel." He looked around to see a blonde by the bar.

"Evening, Bunni." He turned away from her and put his order in with the bartender.

"Two drinks? You have a date tonight? Too bad. I was hoping for a dance." She sidled up to him, rubbed her hand on his arm.

"Um, I'm afraid my dance card is full tonight." He grabbed the drinks, tipped the bartender, and turned to leave. "Take care, Bunni."

This was why he typically didn't come to these events. There were always women like Bunni around who wanted to dance...or more. He'd never been interested in messing with married women, and he had no desire to be with anyone other than Breena tonight. He was telling the truth about his dance card being full. He intended to dance with only one woman.

He looked across the room to watch her talking and laughing with Mrs. Marshall. He appreciated that she wasn't a wallflower and that she seemed to enjoy talking to people. He also appreciated that she could read people.

As if drawn like a magnet, her eyes locked on his. She smiled at him, then returned to her conversation with Gigi. He felt something shift inside him; one of the many locks protecting his heart clicked open. He froze, staring at the back of Breena's head. How the heck had that happened? How had she gotten past his defenses?

Gabriel took an unsettled breath and continued to the table. He set Breena's drink in front of her. "I'm going to sit by Tom for a few minutes. Need to talk business."

"No problem. Thanks for the drink."

Mrs. Marshall leaned over and whispered to Breena. Breena looked up at him with a funny expression on her face, then turned back to Mrs. Marshall and their conversation.

The crowd clapped as the presentation finished, and the staff started clearing some of the tables out of the middle of the room for the dance floor.

"I can understand why you support this foundation," Breena said, leaning closer. "It sounds like they do amazing work."

"Yeah, if they can find a way to help Carly, or others with traumatic brain injuries, live life a little better, I'm happy to support them."

She patted the green ribbon on his chest and smiled at him then turned back to the stage.

"I hope you're up for some dancing tonight," he whispered in her ear. "It's all that's been keeping me going tonight. The thought that I get to hold you in my arms and dance with you."

She turned her head to look at him. He could feel her breath on his cheek. "I think I can spare a dance for you. Though I have to tell you, I did promise to dance with someone else."

He was stunned. He could feel the caveman inside him beating his chest in protest. "You promised someone else a dance? But you're here with me?" His heart clenched. Of course he didn't have any real claim to her. But she was *his* date tonight.

When did dating Breena become real? he wondered.

Just then, Tom interrupted. "You ready for our dance, Miss O'Malley?" He winked at Gabriel.

Mrs. Marshall leaned over and smiled at him. "Take a deep breath, Gabriel, then ask me to dance with you."

Feeling chagrined, he stood up and held out his hand, and they walked to the dance floor together.

"I like your young lady. She suits you very well."

"What do you mean, she 'suits' me?" Gabriel was curious.

"You're much calmer when she's around. Well...except when you thought she'd be dancing with someone else." She chuckled. "You looked like you were ready to commit murder until you saw it was my Tom."

He wasn't sure what to say. He'd always prided himself on hiding his feelings, on his poker face. But it didn't sound like he'd hid it very well tonight.

"Do me a favor, Gabriel? Break in with Breena so I can dance with my husband."

"Why, Mrs. Marshall, you're nothing but a matchmaker, aren't you?"

"It might have been a few years since I was young and in love, but I recognize it." She must have felt his body stiffen at that comment because she patted his arm. "It'll be okay, Gabriel. Take it as slow as you need to."

Chapter 15

BREENA

"You watch." Tom chuckled. "He'll be steering Gigi over here within a minute. She's a matchmaker and just can't help herself."

Breena laughed as she watched Gabe guide Mrs. Marshall straight to where she and Tom were dancing.

"Mind if I cut in?"

Tom was smooth. He twirled Breena around, directly into Gabe's arms and moved to welcome his wife into his own.

Breena settled into Gabe's embrace. His head rested against the top of hers, and she heard him sigh. Floating around the dance floor with Gabe was everything Breena had dreamed it would be. And yes, she had dreamed about it.

One song led to another and another...and they stayed on the dance floor. He had one arm around her waist and a hand in her own. She discreetly felt his strong shoulder with her other hand. For someone who worked in an office, he certainly seemed to be in excellent shape.

He pulled her a little closer. "This is why we came tonight. I needed an excuse to get you in my arms."

She could feel his cheek on top of her head. It felt so right being in his arms. He made her feel...well, she wasn't really sure. Content? Maybe, except for the tension he also brought. Happy? Maybe, except she didn't really know where she stood with him. What she did know was she hadn't felt like this with any other man she'd gone out with. Not that she was *really* going out with Gabe. What was going to happen when their fake dating was over? It had to be soon. She definitely didn't want to think about it tonight.

Laci had warned her not to fall for Gabe. And she was really trying not to.

Tonight, she wasn't going to worry about any of it. Tonight, she was going to be in the moment. And in this moment, she relished being in Gabe's arms.

At the end of the fourth song, Gabe led her back to the table. She sat next to Mrs. Marshall while they waited for the men to bring them drinks.

"Gabriel certainly seems attentive tonight," Mrs. Marshall observed.

Breena looked over at her. "Is he?"

"Oh yes, my dear. I don't think I've ever seen him dance at one of these events. He's a wonderful dancer."

Breena smiled and nodded at the thought of being in his arms.

"You make a beautiful couple."

"Oh. Well, I don't know that we're a, um, couple." On seeing Mrs. Marshall's frown, she remembered they were fake dating and trying to sell it. Why did life have to be so complicated? She shook her head. "Sorry, this is all so new. Thank you."

Mrs. Marshall smiled at her. "I remember when my Tom and I were dating, it was all very heady and very scary. This year, we're celebrating our fortieth anniversary." She had a dreamy, reminiscing look on her face.

"Wow, forty years. That's amazing. Congratulations." The thought of being with one person for forty years was mind-boggling. "How—" She stopped herself because the question sounded stupid in her head.

Mrs. Marshall seemed to understand. "It's a long time to be with one person, isn't it? It might start out as love, but to keep going for so long, there has to be friendship and commitment. Not nearly as sexy to talk about as love or lust or hormones, but friendship and commitment, along with love, is what makes decades possible."

Breena watched as Mrs. Marshall's eyes tracked her husband as he made his way across the room with Gabe. Yes, there was love in that look. Breena wondered if she would ever have that level of intimacy—of love, friendship, and commitment—with someone. And was it possible with Gabe?

After finishing their drinks and an enjoyable conversation with the Marshalls, Breena and Gabe headed back to the dance floor.

"Mmm, I was ready to be back out here with you," Gabe whispered into her hair. His breath and his words sent a shiver down her back.

"I didn't realize you enjoyed dancing so much." She looked up at him. "Mrs. Marshall said you normally don't dance at these events."

He looked back at her. "Mrs. Marshall said that, did she? Well, she's not wrong. I don't normally dance at these things. I usually just come, talk with who I need to, then leave."

"So what's different tonight?"

"Well..." Gabe took a deep breath. "I guess *you* are what's different."

Breena looked up at him, tilting her head, questioning.

"In case you haven't noticed, I enjoy having you in my arms, Breena."

His look seared her; goosebumps popped up and down her arms. Was she ready for this? Was this even real? But again, she decided she would worry about those questions later.

"That works out nicely because I enjoy being in your arms." She smiled at him, then rested her cheek on his chest. She felt his cheek settle on her hair again, and she was content.

When the song ended, Breena was ready for a break. "How about a quick walk outside?"

"Sure. Want your jacket?"

"No, I'm really warm and just need a quick cooldown." Very soon, she realized not having her jacket was a mistake. It was freezing outside.

Gabe had apparently realized it, too, and draped his tuxedo jacket around her shoulders. "Better?"

"Thanks." She chuckled. "Guess I'm not as tough as I thought. It's freezing out here."

He turned her to face him, and his arms went around her waist, pulling her close. "I'll keep you warm."

Her body immediately flooded with heat. Her heart raced. She looped her arms around his waist and took a deep breath. He smelled like aftershave, wine, and...*Gabe*. She was definitely in trouble with this one. Her heart was at risk, she realized. She hadn't had her heart involved in a relationship in a long time. Her mom had shown her where that would get her.

"You warmer?" Gabe breathed into her hair.

"Mm-hmm." Her cheek rested on his chest, and she listened to his strong heartbeat. Her own heart matched the beat.

She felt his finger under her chin, tipping her head up. She looked into his deep blue eyes. They were intense, focused only on her and nothing else. She felt special and nervous to have his undivided attention like this.

He looked down at her mouth. Her tongue nervously licked her lips. His eyes became even darker.

One of his hands moved from her lower back to the back of her head, his head lowering toward hers.

His eyes were now looking straight into hers. She couldn't look away. She could feel his breath on her lips. He was just a breath away.

Her lips parted a little in invitation. She wanted his mouth on hers. She stood on her toes and closed the gap.

She took the kiss she wanted.

His lips were warm and soft. His tongue teased her lips, then she was open to him and to its exploration. A small groan escaped her lips. Or maybe he groaned. She wasn't sure. She moved her hands up his chest until her arms were around his neck, then tilted her head to take the kiss deeper.

She didn't know if it was seconds later or minutes, but they pulled away from each other, panting, and just stared.

Gabe leaned down, his forehead resting on hers. "I think I'm in trouble."

"Hmm." Breena brought her arms down and rested her hands on his chest.

"Come home with me tonight," he whispered in her ear.

Breena pulled back a couple of inches to look up at him. "I can't do that."

"You are my girlfriend, you know." He gave her a grin.

"*Fake* girlfriend, Gabe. And fake girlfriends don't go home with you. At least this one doesn't. Besides,

I wouldn't do that to Laci. I don't want her to worry about where I am."

Gabe nodded. "Yeah, I get that." He needed to get Laci a new cell phone, he decided. He pulled Breena in tight again, warming her right up. "How about if tomorrow night we go out on our first *real* date? I have the perfect place to take you."

Breena grinned at him. "I'd like that."

Chapter 16

GABRIEL

THE NEXT NIGHT, GABRIEL waited impatiently for Breena to arrive. He was surprised when a little red convertible pulled into his driveway and parked there. Walking down the deep red brick steps, he admired the vehicle as Breena put the top up. He was a fan of sports cars, and Mercedes was a favorite.

"Nice car, Red." He grinned at her. She looked like a celebrity from the fifties with white-framed, cat-eye sunglasses and a colorful scarf covering her hair.

"Thanks. I have to say, I love zipping around the hills in this baby." She stepped out of the car and tossed her sunglasses and scarf on the front seat.

He walked around the car, one hand behind his back, and stopped in front of her. He looked her up and down, grinning. "You look good."

She wore a pair of jeans and a deep purple sweater with heeled, black booties.

He bent his head down, his eyes staying on hers, stopping a millimeter from her lips. "I'm glad you're here." He closed the gap and let his lips settle onto hers. He could feel the tension leave his shoulders. Raising his head, he stepped back. "For you," he said bringing his right hand from behind his back. He held a bouquet of pink tulips, a ribbon wrapped around the stems.

"You remembered," she said softly, her head tilted slightly to the left. She looked up into his eyes. "Thank you, Gabe. These are beautiful."

"They wrapped the bottom so they should be fine until you can put them in a vase later tonight," he said as she put them on the front seat of the car. He grabbed her hand after she locked the doors. "So would you like a tour of Casa van Neugh now or after dinner?"

Breena looked behind him to the townhouse he called home. He followed her gaze and tried to see his building through her eyes. He loved the dark red brick row of townhouses.

"I love this part of town. I haven't spent much time here, but it's beautiful." She smiled and continued looking around. "I'm starving though, so do you mind saving the tour until after dinner?"

He grinned. "No problem. Let's head over now."

Hands linked, they walked across the street and about halfway down the block. She slowed down, stepping carefully, making sure her heels didn't get caught in the sidewalk.

"These probably aren't the best shoes for a brick sidewalk," she commented.

"Hmm. Fortunately, we don't have far to go."

He steered her toward a wooden doorway with Amati's painted in red across it. This was Gabriel's favorite restaurant in Nashville. It was a small, mom-and-pop place with delicious, authentic, Italian food. He came here at least twice a month. The owners, Mr. and Mrs. Amati, were everything you would expect from Italian restaurant owners. They greeted Gabriel by name whenever he came in, knew what he liked to eat, and always treated him like family.

He pulled open the heavy door, and the scent of garlic, tomato, and yeasty bread greeted them. His stomach grumbled in response to the tantalizing aromas, making him realize just how hungry he was.

"Oh my gosh, this smells so good." Breena stepped into the small, cozy restaurant and looked around. Along one wall were painted murals of the Italian countryside. Family pictures, looking like they went back several generations, were scattered around. It always felt like visiting their home instead of a restaurant.

"Gabriel!" Mr. Amati greeted him with enthusiasm, kissing him on both cheeks. "And who is this lovely young lady?" He picked up Breena's hand. "Welcome to Amati's."

"Mr. Amati, may I introduce Breena O'Malley? Breena, this is the one and only Mr. Amati."

Gabriel had never brought a female guest here—well, any guest—so the Amatis fawned over her, making her feel welcome. It warmed his heart that they were treating her special. He wanted this night to be special. He also wanted her to like this restaurant and these people who were important to him.

It had taken a little getting used to, the fact that everyone liked Breena. She was a genuine person, and people seemed to naturally gravitate to her. Typically, his dates were women who were interested in moving up the social ladder by finding a rich husband.

But not Breena.

She was authentically interested in others and listened to what they said. It was one of the first things he'd noticed about her—he'd felt like she really listened to him.

When he'd taken her to that first party at the Marshalls', he hadn't been prepared for people to have an opinion about his date. Several had commented on how much they enjoyed her, and Mrs. Marshall had even said she wanted to see Breena again. He'd never put himself in a position to hear that type of comment before. He wasn't sure how to handle it.

The Amatis hadn't allowed Gabriel or Breena to order. Instead, they said they would treat them to a delicious meal. Breena had been enthusiastic about the idea, but Gabriel wasn't sure. He liked what he liked; why mess with it? He wasn't going to grumble, but this definitely threw him off a bit. It was, after all, their first date.

Well, first *real* date.

Wineglass in hand, Gabriel finished chewing the delicious, fresh-from-the-oven bread Mrs. Amati brought to them. He couldn't remember the last time he'd dined with anyone, prior to Breena, just talking about their days.

But that's exactly what they were doing.

It had been an especially stressful day. He told her how the tour was coming together. He'd spent the day organizing much of the sponsorship and financing tasks. He enjoyed telling her about the problems he'd run into, the people who had frustrated him. It was interesting to hear her take on the different personalities and situations. She looked at the world very differently than he did.

"So how was *your* day?" He rarely asked a date about her day, but he found he genuinely wanted to know how she'd spent the last twenty or so hours away from him.

Before she could answer, his phone rang. "I'm sorry. Do you mind if I take this?"

"No, go ahead."

He stepped outside and talked to one of the finance people.

"So you were about to tell me about your day?" He settled back into his seat, enjoying his wine and listening to Breena share about her day. The light Irish lilt of her voice calmed him in a way that nothing else could.

Mrs. Amati bustled over with a large bowl of pasta and two plates. "We do family style tonight, yes." She informed rather than asked as she topped off their wines. "Enjoy. Enjoy."

"I don't think it's possible to *not* enjoy this," Breena said through a mouthful of pasta. She closed her eyes, and her face looked rapturous.

Watching her enjoy her food chipped at something deep inside Gabriel. It was another thing past dates never did, enjoy food. His dates usually ordered a salad but rarely ate much of it. He really liked a woman who enjoyed eating, he discovered.

"Mm-hmm," Gabriel agreed with his mouth full. "This is even better than my normal order. And that's saying something. I may have to bring you more often."

Breena raised an eyebrow but didn't comment.

Gabriel's phone rang, taking him away from the moment, yet again. "I'm sorry," he said, looking into her eyes, but this time he turned off the ringer and put the phone in his pocket, out of sight. He saw her raise an eyebrow, but neither said anything. He couldn't remember the last time he'd ignored his phone.

It was cold and windy outside, but they were warm and cocooned in the cozy restaurant. He sat watching Breena laugh at something Mr. Amati said and felt another click in the neighborhood of his heart. Seeing her enjoy herself seemed to make his heart expand.

Dinner wound up being three courses, plus dessert. After the pasta came a fish dish, and the third dish was roasted vegetables with a reduced balsamic sauce. Gabriel had never been a fan of brussels sprouts, but these were delicious. It was a long, leisurely, delicious meal. The Amatis had outdone themselves, and both he and Breena had thoroughly enjoyed it.

"How about we take a walk around the neighborhood to work off some of that meal?" he proposed.

She groaned a little. "More like a waddle around the neighborhood. But yes, that's a really good idea."

He paid the check, and they each received hugs from both Mr. and Mrs. Amati on their way out.

"Gabriel, you bring this one back. I like her," Mrs. Amati said.

He nodded that he would, and they stepped out into the chilly night.

If Gabriel had to describe his feelings in this moment, he would have to say content.

Fully content.

He couldn't think of the any time in the last ten years he'd felt that way. Content was not something he strived for. Successful, yes; content, no. A brief niggle in the back of his brain had him wondering if he had things backward, but he quickly shut the thought down.

After helping her into her jacket, Gabriel linked their hands when they got outside. He liked the idea of showing her a piece of his world and led her down these brick sidewalks of Germantown that he knew so well. He told her about the different restaurants and stores he'd visited since moving here four years earlier. They made it nearly two blocks before he felt his phone vibrate in his pocket. He pulled it out and looked at the number..

"Shoot." Gabriel looked at Breena. "I'm really sorry. I've been waiting on this particular call all day."

"It's okay, Gabe. Go. Take your call, then come back and tell me more about your neighborhood." She smiled at him.

He stepped into a doorway to hear a little better while Breena walked around, looking in shop windows.

A minute into his call, Breena's scream tore through the night.

Phone call forgotten, heart beating double-time, Gabriel raced around the corner to find Breena.

Chapter 17

BREENA

BREENA STAYED STILL ON the sidewalk, trying not to think about all the gross things she was lying on as she assessed her situation. The pain was staggering. Her head throbbed, and she could feel a bump swelling on the left side of it. Swelling was good, she reminded herself. The palms of her hands were bloody and torn up, dirt and bits of gravel embedded in her palms from trying to catch herself. She mentally worked her way down her body and realized the worst pain was coming from her right ankle.

A lot of pain there.

Gabe tore around the corner and was down on the sidewalk next to her within seconds. "What happened? Are you okay?" His face was pale, his eyes wide, but he carefully looked her over. He took hold of her hands, then loosened his grip when he realized they were bloody and hurt.

"Some guy knocked into me. My heel got caught between some of the bricks, and I fell. Hard. I think something is wrong with my right ankle." Breena closed her eyes and took a deep breath as a wave of pain rolled through her. "I need to have it looked at."

Gabe briefly looked around, as if maybe trying to find the person who had done this to her. "Do I need to call an ambulance? Or are you okay going to my car?"

"Your car is fine. I just need to be careful of my ankle."

He nodded at that, took his keys out, and handed them to her.

"Um, you know I can't drive, right?"

He looked at her with an eyebrow raised. "I thought you might be able to unlock the doors." With that, he reached under her knees and arms and lifted her off the ground.

"Oh!" Her left arm immediately went around his neck. She'd never before been whisked off her feet by a man. It was an incredibly intimate experience. She laid her head on his shoulder, trying to block out the pain that came with every other step. He carried her across the street to where he'd parked his car behind his house and waited as she unlocked the doors. Then, gently setting her on her good leg and keeping an arm around her, he opened the passenger door.

She put her right foot down for support, and the pain was dizzying. She grabbed Gabe's shirt just before her world went black.

Breena heard the beeps and buzzes before opening her eyes. The hospital noises were all too familiar to her, being a nurse for the past ten years. Slowly, she opened her eyes. The first thing to come into focus was Gabe's concerned face.

He was looking out the window, rubbing his hands across his stubbled cheek. His face was pale when he looked at her.

"Hey." He rushed over to the bed and took her right hand gently in his. Wondering why she couldn't feel anything, she looked down to see her hand wrapped in gauze. It looked like a mummy. "You're awake."

"Kinda." She found her voice hoarse, her throat dry. "What happened?"

"You blacked out on me" he said, letting out a shaky breath and looking around the room. "They were able clean you up. You've got a bump on your head, but they didn't seem to think you had a concussion. And your ankle still needs something...I can't remember what they said though. I called Carl and Grace, so they know what's going on. I didn't want

anyone to freak out when you didn't come home."
He took a deep breath. "I'm sorry. I'm babbling. You
worried me." He sat down heavily in the chair next
to her bed, still holding her hand, and looked around
the room. "This freaks me out. I haven't been in a
hospital in years,"

"Water?" she asked, having a hard time keeping
him in focus.

"Oh right, of course." He found a cup with a
straw and filled it, then held it to her lips so she could
ease her dry throat.

She lay back with her eyes closed. "Thank you."

Just then, Grace rushed in. "Oh my gosh, what
happened? Are you okay?" She looked from Breena to
Gabe and back to Breena. She went to the other side
of the bed and picked up her other wrapped hand.

Breena tried to nod, but it hurt her head. "I'll be
okay, Grace. Just banged up a bit."

Grace looked over Breena to Gabe. "What happened, Gabriel?"

"I was on a call and heard her scream. When I got
to her, she was on the ground. She had a bump on her
head, blood on her hands, and a sore, swollen ankle.
She passed out when I was getting her into my car to
bring her here."

Breena noticed sweat beading on his upper lip
and that he was getting a little pale. "Hey, are you
okay?"

"I, uh...I need to get out of here." With that, he
stood up and bolted for the door.

Grace looked from the doorway to Breena. "Wonder what that was about? I hope he's okay."

"I think he just needs fresh air. I don't think he has fond memories of hospitals. It's hard for some people." Breena had seen it before, many times as a nurse. But she missed Gabe being here with her. "Could you sit my bed up a bit, please?"

Grace nodded and got her situated. "I'm grateful he stayed with you until I got here." She looked at the doorway for a second, then back to Breena. "So what happened, Bree?"

"I'm not completely sure. I was just walking along, looking in shop windows while Gabe was on the phone...and someone rushed past me, bumping into me. My heel got caught in the brick sidewalk, and I went down. I must have screamed. After that, I don't really remember much until waking here a couple of minutes ago." She had a flash of being in Gabe's arms, his scent surrounding her, and a feeling of safety.

"I'm grateful he got you here and stayed with you. After that reaction, I'm surprised he didn't just call an ambulance versus bringing you here himself," Grace said.

Breena frowned. She knew Gabe hated hospitals, so the fact that he had stuck with her meant something, but it hurt her head trying to think through it.

"Oh, I went by the apartment to make sure everything was okay." She gave Breena a pointed look. Breena knew she wouldn't mention Laci here, but she was glad Grace had checked on her. "I grabbed a few things I thought you might need."

For the first time, Breena noticed a bag on the floor next to Grace.

"I didn't grab much. Hairbrush. Toothbrush. PJs and leggings and a sweater. I wasn't sure what you'd need." She pulled things out of the bag as she named them.

Breena smiled at her. "Hopefully, I won't be here too long. Gabe didn't mention when they'd let me out."

The next time she woke up, it was bright outside. Gabe was sitting next to her bed, reading a book, and a nurse was checking her chart.

"Good morning." The nurse bustled over to check her. "How're you feeling?"

Gabe looked up at the comment and was immediately on his feet and next to the bed.

"I feel like I was up close and personal with a brick sidewalk. Ugh." She looked at Gabe. "You're here?" It was an exclamation, but also a question.

He smiled a little sheepishly. "Yeah, I needed to make sure you're okay. And Grace looked like she could use a break. Sorry I ran out last night."

"No problem. Thank you for getting me here. I really appreciate it." She looked back at the nurse. "May I see my chart?" The nurse seemed taken aback at Breena's request. "I'm a nurse, and I'd like to see what's been going on with me since I got here."

The nurse reluctantly handed over the chart and continued checking Breena over. "Looks like your blood pressure's still good," the nurse mumbled under her breath. "I'd like to take the bandages off your hands and see how they're looking."

Breena nodded and handed the chart back. "Thanks. It's hard to be the one on this end of care." She grinned wryly at the nurse.

"Yeah, I can imagine. The bump on your head seems to be good. We were a little concerned about a concussion, but the doctor cleared that this morning. They got the X-rays on your ankle. Looks like nothing's broken, just a bad bruise. You lucked out there"

Breena let out a breath. "Oh thank goodness. I was really concerned about that."

"The doc will be in soon to chat about it. They should let you go home today, assuming you have someone who can help you. You'll want to stay off that foot for a couple of days." She looked at Gabe.

"Oh...sure. I'm happy to help."

"She'll need help getting dressed and undressed, showering, washing her hair, and of course, cooking and cleaning."

Breena laughed at Gabe's eyes getting bigger with each new thing. "Grace can help me with most of that."

"Sorry, I thought just bringing a meal would be helpful. Though I'm happy to help with some of that other stuff." He gave her a wolfish grin.

The nurse looked from Breena to Gabe. "Oh sorry. I assumed you were together...with you being here all night, I guess I just thought..." She faded out.

Breena saw Gabe's neck getting red.

"We were on our first date when this happened," she told the nurse, laughing. "A little too new for some of that stuff."

The thought of Gabe helping her in the shower was appealing. She could feel her own face getting warm.

Her hospital stay lasted almost twenty-four hours. Breena was thankful for the clean clothes Grace had brought, but she wasn't able to wear the leggings. So her going-home outfit consisted of pajama pants, a clean sweater, and hospital socks. Gabe had stuck with her throughout the day, with Grace popping in during the morning to make sure all was going well.

They wheeled her to the covered pickup spot where Gabe's car was waiting. He helped her out of the wheelchair and into the front seat of his car. After getting her in the seat and helping her buckle her seat belt, he gave her a lingering kiss before ducking back out of the car. Breena flushed a little seeing the nurse's smile.

Her right ankle was in a soft cast to protect it for the next couple of days. Gabe stuck her crutches in the -, then walked around the to driver's seat.

"I have to tell you, I'm really happy you're not passed out this trip." He looked at her before shifting the car into drive. "So does this count as our second date?"

Breena laughed despite everything that had happened in the last twenty-four hours. She'd never broken a bone before and was very grateful that was still true. "I'm happy to count this as a second date. And thank you for coming back to the hospital. I know it wasn't where you wanted to be."

"I hadn't been in a hospital since my parents died," he said softly. "Carly was in there for so long. Being there last night brought back a lot of hard memories. I've tried to forget that period in my life. I guess it doesn't work like that."

Breena squeezed his arm. "It's even more impressive then that you stuck with me until Grace got there. Even though I was out of it most of that time, I appreciate that yours was the first face I saw when I woke up."

"I was so relieved when you opened your eyes. It was like I could finally breathe. When Grace showed up, it was like I finally had permission to freak out." He laughed a little. "That doesn't make sense, does it?"

"You came back though. Why did you come back?"

"I went to see Carly last night after I left the hospital and told her about your accident so she'd know why you weren't able to visit her for a little while. They've told me she has the brain of a nine-year-old, but sometimes, I think she is one of the smartest people I know." He smiled tenderly. "I told her I didn't think I would be able to go back to the hospital to see you, but she told me I needed to. She said each time we do something really hard, it gets a little easier. And if I went back today, it would be a little easier than it was last night."

Breena's eyes teared up at Carly's wise words. "Your sister is very special, you know that right?"

He stole a quick glance at her and nodded. "I do. She might be different than other twenty-year-olds, but she has a great perspective on life. She reminds me constantly of what's important. I'm glad I came back to the hospital last night because she was right. It *was* a little easier."

Breena smiled. They swung by a pharmacy on their way to the penthouse to pick up Breena's prescriptions. Fortunately, it had been called in and they were able to go through the drive-through.

"Want anything else before we head to your place? Food?"

"No, I'm good, but thank you." She was anxious to get home to relax in her own space. Even though she couldn't do much, she needed the comfort of home right now.

The elevator doors opened, and Gabe helped her into the apartment. Grace and Laci both jumped to their feet, offering to help, but Gabe easily lifted her into his arms, carried her into the living room, and settled her on the couch. He put pillows behind her back and under her foot before hovering like a mother hen.

"Do you mind grabbing my crutches and purse from your car?" Breena asked.

"Oh, sure..." He hesitated a minute. "Are you sure you're okay here?"

"Um, Gabe. You know *we* are here, right?" Laci stood behind him with her hands on her hips. "I'm pretty sure we can handle anything that comes up." She said it gently but walked him to the elevator.

As soon as the doors closed, Breena leaned back on the pillow and sighed. "He's been so sweet, but I'm ready for you two." Gabe had been wonderful, but now she needed the comfort of home and girlfriends. But even as she thought it, she already missed Gabe's presence.

Grace gently hugged her. "Don't worry. We'll move him along so you can relax."

Laci was right behind Grace and gave Breena a hug too. "I've been so worried. I'm really glad you let me stay, so now *I* can help *you*."

Breena had been right. Coming home was exactly what she needed—home and friends.

Chapter 18

GABRIEL

GABRIEL COULDN'T BELIEVE THEY kicked him out. He supposed they were right—Breena did need her rest. And he really didn't need to watch her sleep. Though if he were being honest, he *enjoyed* watching her sleep. But he left them to take care of her, knowing they cared about her as much as he did.

As he pulled into his driveway, he saw Breena's bright red convertible still in the driveway. With all the chaos of the last twenty-four hours, he'd forgotten it. At some point, he'd have to get it back to her, but for the moment, it felt good having it in one of his parking spaces. Almost like he was coming home to her.

He paused at that. He'd never wanted to come home to anyone, except maybe Carly. He was surprised, though, how good the thought made him feel.

He ran up the brick steps to his front door. Walking in, he waited for the sense of comfort that always came with being in his space. He bought the townhouse four years ago, when he was finally making enough to afford the mortgage. Since then, he'd purchased all five of the townhouses in his building and rented the others out.

He headed up the stairs to his bedroom and kicked off his shoes. He didn't want to be alone here, so Gabriel changed into running clothes and headed out the door. With each block, tension left his shoulders as he pounded down the sidewalks. While he worried about Breena, he knew she was in good hands.

More than anything, he realized he missed her. He'd been with her for more than twenty-four hours almost straight, and he liked being around her. He'd never missed a girl before, except his sister.

This was new territory for him. Scary territory.

"Gabriel." He heard his name and slowed to a stop, looking around. Mr. Amati waved to him from the doorway of his restaurant across the street. Gabe smiled and waved before crossing the street.

"Mr. Amati, how are you?"

"Where is your lovely lady? We enjoyed meeting her last night."

Gabriel told him about Breena hurting her ankle only a couple of blocks away, shortly after leaving the restaurant the night before.

"I just dropped her off at her apartment downtown. She's in good hands with a couple of girlfriends taking care of her." He didn't share that he'd been kicked out. "I was thinking about getting some takeout, but I don't have my wallet on me."

"You finish your run, get changed, come back. Then we feed you. Yes?"

Gabriel smiled. It would be nice to be with friends tonight. Might help take his mind off Breena. So he agreed and said he'd be back in about forty minutes.

Forty-five minutes later, feeling refreshed and relaxed, Gabriel walked into Amati's. The scent of garlic and bread surrounded him. It felt like home.

Mrs. Amati made her way over to him with a worried look on her face. "Is she okay? Your Breena? Luca told me about the accident."

He followed her to a table near the kitchen, and she sat down across from him. Mr. Amati deposited a basket of garlic bread and a carafe of house red wine before pulling up a chair to join them. If Gabriel thought he'd get through the evening without thinking about Breena, he was mistaken. The Amatis wanted to hear all about her. How did they meet? How long had they been dating?

Gabriel poured three glasses of wine and settled in for a long conversation. He considered the couple friends and wanted to share with them what had happened. At least, as much as he could without mentioning Laci.

"So Breena is not your lady? Only fake dating?" Mrs. Amati asked, confused. "That can't be right. I see the way you two look at each other. There is love there."

Gabriel's heart skipped a beat at the L-word. It wasn't part of his vocabulary in his dating life. "Well, last night was our first *real* date. Guess it was a memorable first date." His voice was a little shaky as he thought about Mrs. Amati's comments. When had life become so complicated?

Fake dating.

Real dating.

Love?

Since he hadn't been able to share about Laci, he said he needed a date for a few work-related outings, and Breena had agreed to go with him as a pretend date. The Amatis didn't really understand it, but it wasn't to be helped tonight; Laci was still in hiding. Maybe one day he'd be able to explain it all a little better.

The waiter brought over three bowls of pasta e fagioli soup, refilled their wine glasses, and left them to it. Gabriel found the soup perfectly hit the spot. It was exactly what he'd been craving, and he hadn't even known it. And like everything else here, it was delicious. The spicy tomato broth, the veggies with a little bite, the beans and pasta—it all made the perfect comfort food. Tonight, he was in need of comfort food.

"So when will you be seeing your Breena again?" Mrs. Amati wanted to know.

"I was thinking of taking some flowers to her to-morrow after work. I just want to make sure she's okay."

Mrs. Amati nodded her head approvingly.

And while his excuse was true, he also found he was having a hard time staying away from her.

He spent the rest of the meal sharing details about the tour he was organizing, some of the new acts they hoped to sign and bring with them. And they shared stories of their family in Italy, some of the current restaurant drama, catching him up on their children. It felt like a family meal. Spending time sharing stories with people you genuinely enjoy. While he'd always enjoyed coming in here, it had never been like this.

It felt like Breena was bringing more into his life without even being here. Another one of the locks protecting his heart clicked open.

Chapter 19

BREENA

Dear Ms. O'Malley,

I am utterly flabbergasted at these results!

I'd hoped to hear from you by now, but maybe you're still processing...

Patiently waiting,

Peter

Dear Mr. Simmonds,

I apologize for not responding sooner. I wound up in the hospital for a night, and it's taken me a few days to catch back up with life.

Anyway, I'm hoping that "utterly flabbergasted" is a good thing?

I am thrilled with the results. When I sent that first email to you, I was angry you had rejected me my whole life. Now, I'm hoping you want a relationship with your daughter! That's so crazy to say—your daughter!

I hope you are pleased, and I hope you'll call me Breena.

Your daughter,

Breena

"**G**OOD MORNING." LACI POKED her head into the living room.

"Morning," Breena grumbled. She'd wound up sleeping on the chair in the living room because she was able to keep her foot elevated and protected while leaning back to get somewhat comfortable. It had proved to be a better sleeping situation than either her bed or the couch.

"I'll get some coffee going then help you into the bathroom." Laci had offered to help her shower this morning and then get dressed. It was humbling to ask for help for even the simplest of tasks, Breena realized. It certainly gave her new empathy for her patients.

"Okay, thanks." She grimaced as she removed the pillows from under and around her foot before lowering the footrest to get organized to stand up.

An hour later, freshly showered and dressed in soft black palazzo pants and a long dark-green sweater, Breena sat at the dining room table with a cup of coffee and a bagel. Her ankle was propped up on a chair with a pillow, and she was beginning to feel somewhat human again.

She found that as long as her leg was up, it wasn't as painful. Which made it pretty much impossible to do anything. The disappointment of not being able to attend Grace's wedding dress appointment was almost as painful as her ankle. They had been planning this since Grace's engagement Christmas morning.

"So I was talking to Grace last night," Laci started.

Breena, already feeling left out, could sense resentment edging in. She took a bite of her bagel to avoid having to say anything, but she looked at Laci.

"We decided it was completely unfair you won't be able to go to the wedding dress appointment today, so I suggested she move it here so you can still be part of the day."

The news was so unexpected, Breena just stared at Laci. She felt tears prickling, and the lump in her throat made it hard to speak. "I..." She took a deep breath. She felt horrible that her first reaction had been resentment of Laci talking to Grace. The tears were trailing down her cheeks. She could see Laci wasn't sure how to respond, so she reached over to take Laci's hand while she wiped her face with a napkin.

"Thank you so much, Laci. I was just thinking how miserable it was going to be to miss it. I can't believe you were able to arrange to have it here."

Laci smiled a little wryly. "With enough money, you can make just about anything happen. But seriously, it didn't seem fair for you to miss it. I'm guessing it will be really hard for you to move around much today. It seems like having your leg propped up is the most comfortable position, and that would make it challenging to be out and about. But they were willing to come here for Grace to try her dresses on. It'll be fun."

Breena realized in that moment just how close Laci had become to her and her little circle of friends. She'd not become friends with any of the women who'd come through the safe house thus far, but Laci was different. Not only was Gabe part of the picture with her, but she also seemed to just slide into step with Breena, Grace, and Jillian.

Laci continued, "So as soon as Grace and Jillian get here, I'll head over to the other apartment and stay out of the way."

"Wait. What?" Breena's head shot around so she could look at Laci, which caused stars to pop out in front of her. She closed her eyes until her vision settled, then tried again. "Why would you do that?"

"Well, I don't want to be in the way of you and your friends," Laci said softly, looking at her hands.

"Well, that's the silliest thing I've ever heard. Of course you'll be here, Lace. You're one of us now. You know that, right?"

"I appreciate it, but this is Grace's big day. I don't want to intrude."

"You are anything but an intruder, Lace. You've become a friend. I was just thinking how I hadn't become friends with any of the other women who've come through the safe house. I haven't stayed in touch with any of them. But I hope *we* stay in touch when you leave."

Laci sniffed. "Thank you," she said softly. "I enjoy you, Grace, and Jilly. I don't have a lot of girlfriends...I have a ton of acquaintances, but not many friends." She gave Breena a watery smile.

Breena laughed. "Look at us, a couple of blubbering women this morning."

Just then, the buzzer went off.

Breena saw Laci stiffen a bit. "You know it's not Hank, right?"

"Yeah, just a habit, I guess. Mind if I answer?"

"That'd be great, thanks."

Gabe walked through the elevator doors a few minutes later. He had a huge bouquet, a box of chocolates, and a teddy bear.

"Gifts for the invalid." He smiled, walking past Laci to give Breena a kiss on the cheek. She blushed and saw Laci's eyebrow lift.

"That's very sweet. Thank you. Think you could help me back over to the chair in the living room?"

"And then you're going to have to leave," said Laci. "We have girl things going on today. Girl things that won't include you."

Breena bit her lip to keep from laughing at the look on Gabe's face.

"Girl things?"

"Grace is trying on wedding dresses here today instead of at the shop. So you'll need to shove off pretty quickly." As Laci spoke, the elevator doors opened again, and Grace and Jillian walked in.

He leaned in close to Breena as he helped her into her chair. "Mind if I call later?" he asked softly, running his finger down her cheek.

Her cheeks colored again, and she nodded.

"Okay, ladies, I'm off. Have fun with your *girl things*." He winked at Breena and was off.

Laci looked at Breena again. "Okay, we need to talk. I want to know what's going on with you and Gabe. First the hospital—I happen to know he hates hospitals. Now gifts and kisses. What gives?"

Grace and Jillian stopped and looked from one to the other. "Ooh, sounds like we got here just in time, Grace," Jillian said.

"I think we need to pull up a chair and catch up. Breena, the floor is all yours." Grace laughed.

Breena's neck was hot, and she could feel the heat creeping up her face.

Laci came over and sat with them. "Well?"

"Sunday was our first real date. Gabe told me Saturday night at the charity event, he'd like to go on a real date. So—"

"He asked you on a real date?" Laci looked flummoxed. "But you're just fake dating until I'm out in the world again."

Breena had always had questions about Laci and Gabe's relationship, and Laci's reaction was bringing those questions up again.

Jillian, never one to worry about propriety, jumped in, looking pointedly at Laci. "Is there a problem with Bree and Gabriel dating?"

"Well, no," she said slowly. "I'm just not sure it's the best idea for either of them."

Grace looked at Laci, her brow furrowed. "Why's that? Is there something between you and Gabriel she should know about?"

"What? No." Laci shook her head. "No. Gabe's just a really good friend. We've known each other since elementary school, and I guess I'm kind of protective of...well, of both of you." She looked at Breena. "He's never been a relationship guy. His business and his sister have always been his priorities. I'd hate for you to get your hopes up and think this might go somewhere."

Breena wasn't sure what to even say. Thankfully, the elevator buzzer broke the tension. The women from the wedding dress boutique had arrived and were on their way up.

But now Breena didn't know what to think about Gabe.

The next hour was spent getting the penthouse organized for the wedding dress party. A catered lunch was delivered and set up in the kitchen. Champagne and non-alcoholic sparkling cider were also delivered. And the boutique ladies came with several racks of dresses. They designated the office as a dressing room then set up a small stage in the living room for Grace to stand on to show off the dresses. They arranged two 3-panel mirrors near the small stage area. All in all, it came together quite well, and Breena enjoyed watching the activity, grateful she was able to be part of this important tradition.

In the back of her mind, she was having a hard time letting go of what Laci said about not getting her hopes up in this relationship. *Well, too late for that*, she realized.

"Okay, ladies, this is going to be fun." Kathy, the boutique owner, was organized and committed to helping Grace find the perfect dress. She rubbed her hands together. "I think we should pour some champagne first, and then we'll jump right in." Her assistant handed out champagne glasses—sparkling cider for Breena, because of her medicine. "A toast to the bride, ladies."

"To Grace. Cheers!" They all smiled and raised their glasses.

Grace was glowing today, Breena noticed. Love looked good on her.

Kathy and Grace went into the office-dressing room to choose the first dress she thought would look good on Grace.

"Okay, everyone close your eyes. Dress number one is coming out." Kathy led Grace to the small stage and set her up in front of the mirrors, fixing the dress and the train. "And open your eyes."

"Ooh, Grace, you're a vision," Breena said. Grace, standing on the makeshift stage, looked like a sweet confection. The skirt was made of layers and layers of tulle, and the fitted white satin bodice was covered with lovely beadwork. The top looked like it was made for her.

Breena looked at her closely. "You get first thoughts, Grace. What do you think?"

"It's beautiful, but not *my* dress."

The ladies nodded their heads.

"But I love the top part of this one."

Kathy nodded and hustled her off to change into the next dress. This went on for seven dresses. Parts of them were exactly right, but not the whole dress.

"Okay, ladies, eyes closed for this next one." Kathy led Grace to the stage, facing the mirrors, and made sure the dress lay perfectly around her. "And open."

There was a stunned silence for a few seconds. Grace's eyes went wide. "Oh my gosh," she whispered. "This is it. This is *my* dress."

It was nothing like any of the dresses she'd previously tried on. The bodice was fitted to the hips, giving a twenties feel to the dress. The wide set straps began in a gentle V between her breasts and extended to the cap of each shoulder, showing off Grace's sculpted arms. The skirt was light and flowy with an asymmetrical top layer. It looked like something Grace Kelly might have worn. The off-white, almost cream fabric complimented Grace's skin tone, and the style accentuated her long, lean body.

Breena's eyes had tears in the corners. "Oh my gosh, Grace. You look amazing. You're a bride!"

"Carl is going to need CPR when he sees you." Jillian was smiling. "Wow, I just realized you're going to be my sister."

They each grabbed a champagne flute and gathered around Breena, toasting to the camera Kathy held.

Dear Breena (I am pleased to call you Breena),

My goodness! I hope you're okay after your hospital stay. And yes, utterly flabbergasted is most assuredly a good thing—haha.

I'm thrilled to call you my daughter, Breena.

When my wife, Cindy, and I were told we couldn't have children, we were crushed. We debated adopting, but well, it wasn't able to happen.

In case you'd like to know a little more about me...

- *I grew up in Cleveland, Ohio*

- *Went to college in Columbus*

- *I'd just graduated with a teaching degree when I met your mother. I was home for the summer (in Cleveland)*

- *I was a high school math teacher for thirty years*

- *I currently live in Phoenix, Arizona*

I'd love to hear more about you.

Proud to be your father,

Peter (and please call me Peter)

Chapter 20

GABRIEL

THE MORNING FLEW BY for Gabriel. As much as he wanted to sit and think about Breena, work demanded all of his attention. He quickly remembered why he didn't have time for relationships.

Kelly walked in with several stacks of papers and files in her arms. "Okay, these need your signature." She set down one stack of files. "These just need you to look through and make any necessary changes." She put another stack down next to the first. "And these"—she set a pile of phone messages on his desk—"are your phone messages. There are only a couple that need a return call."

Gabriel looked at the new pile of work on his desk and let out a sigh. "Thanks, Kelly. We're getting there."

The tour was coming together, slowly but surely. They'd been working toward this for two years, and now it was becoming a reality. The first leg would be thirty concert dates in Asia, and then after a couple of months break, they would have another thirty concert dates in Europe. It was going to be a long, hard several months, but it would take Laci Love to the next level of stardom. They'd been planning for this moment their whole careers.

The two pieces—or people—Gabriel hadn't figured out yet were Carly and Breena. He couldn't leave his sister for that long, and taking her with him around the world wasn't an option. He had a few months to figure it out, but he wasn't yet sure what the answer would be. And Breena...well their relationship was so new, he didn't even know how to navigate it. He'd talk it through with Laci, and maybe even Breena, and see what their thoughts were.

Gabriel stood up and looked down on the city that had become his home. The sun was shining but he knew from his run earlier that morning it was cold and windy. His followed the steely river as it wound its way through the city, small whitecaps forming in the wind.

He thought about the confused look on Laci's face when he brought Breena the gifts and kissed her on the cheek. He knew he probably should have had a conversation with her so she wasn't surprised, but he honestly hadn't thought about it until after. Before going to the penthouse that morning, his brain had been only on Breena. This was a new one for him to think about.

Work, Carly, and Laci—they always came first.

Always.

He wasn't sure he knew how to handle this type of relationship, and he wasn't even sure they were in a relationship. He and Breena certainly hadn't talked about boundaries or expectations. They'd barely gotten through their first date.

He shot off a text to Laci—to the new phone he'd given her—asking her call him when she had a moment. He needed to deal with this sooner rather than later. Laci was important to him.

An hour later, Kelly poked her head in to let him know Laci was on the line and she was headed out to grab a late lunch.

"Okay, see you in a while. Enjoy your lunch." He watched her leave as he picked up the phone. "Laci, how was your girly morning?" he asked with a smile.

"It was a lot of fun. Grace's dress is amazing. She'll make a stunning bride."

"Glad you had a good morning. Listen, we have a few things we need to talk about. Any chance you can drop by the office this afternoon?"

"Sure, I'll swing by after we get everything cleaned up here."

Two hours later, Laci walked in, sporting the brunette pixie-cut wig. He did a double take to make sure it was her. He was curious about why she was still hiding from the media in a wig but didn't question her.

"Let's go to the conference room." He stood up as she came in. After a quick hug, he followed her to the bigger room. "There are a few things we need to go over," he said as he set several files on the table. "But first, I owe you an apology."

"An apology? For what?"

"For not giving you a heads-up about me and Bree."

"I'm pretty sure you've never run your dates by me before. Besides, you and Bree fake dating was my idea."

"This is different, Lace." His voice was soft but strong. "I don't want to *fake* date anymore. This is the first time I've wanted a relationship versus just a date. Breena is different."

Laci was quiet for a moment. "A relationship. Wow. That's...that's great, Gabe." Her voice was a little unsteady.

He wasn't sure what to make of her comment. While she'd said the right thing, something felt off.

They spent the next two hours going through the contracts and the schedule. He'd signed the three of the groups they auditioned and split them up over the tour.

"Oh, that'll be fun having them along. I've been watching videos and listening to each of them. I think this will be great for the tour and their careers."

After finishing up each contract, going through all the details they'd organized thus far, Gabriel brought up his concerns about Carly.

"I know I can't leave her for that long. I don't want to. But I'm not sure what the answer is. Curious if you have any thoughts on it?"

Laci thought for a few minutes. "I can certainly understand why you can't and shouldn't leave Carly," she said. "She's your priority, Gabe. Always has been and always will be."

Gabriel nodded. He appreciated that Laci had been through everything with him. She knew exactly what his priorities were.

"I have two thoughts. One is to take advantage of Breena." She winced a little at how it sounded. "Sorry, that came out wrong. I guess what I mean is, Bree already has a relationship with Carly and she's a nurse. Maybe she can be part of the answer."

Gabriel nodded as he thought about it. "Hmm, I hadn't thought of that. I'll mull it over."

"And my second thought, something you've mentioned several times over the years, is to get a partner. Someone you trust to take part of the tour so you can be home when you need to be."

"I don't—" Gabriel's knee-jerk response was to say he didn't need, or even want, a partner. But he wasn't sure it was true anymore. "Actually, I might be ready to consider that idea."

"Really? I wasn't expecting that answer." Laci's eyes were wide with surprise.

"Yeah." He laughed. "I wasn't either. I was completely prepared to say 'I don't need a partner.' But I think I do. There's enough business to support two of us, easily. Yeah..." His voice faded out. He was thinking it would be nice to be able to have time to give to Breena, but he wasn't prepared to share that. The idea that he wanted his life to include someone else was still very new to him. He was still trying to figure out what it even meant.

They wrapped up their meeting, and Gabriel gathered up the files and headed out of the conference room with Laci on his heels. "It's coming together nicely, isn't it?" Gabriel commented.

"It is. Some of those locations have been on my bucket list my whole life. This is a dream tour you're putting together, Gabriel."

"When are you going to be ready to face the world again?" he asked, cautiously touching her wig.

She avoided his eyes. "Soon. I'm hoping Hank's arrest will be old news soon."

"People are wondering why you haven't shown your face. There's no hurry, though" he said quickly at seeing her expression.

"I know," she said softly. "It'll be soon. I promise. I'm enjoying the break. And I've written so many songs already."

"Can't wait to hear them." He hugged her, smiling after her as she headed out the door.

Chapter 21

BREENA

Dear Peter,

I didn't know you were in Arizona. I spent some time there a few years ago. Beautiful area.

I grew up in central Florida, the Orlando area. Mom—Maeve—left there when I was nine. I'm not sure where she went. My best friend Grace's family took me in and raised me.

I got my nursing degree and spent eight years as a traveling nurse. It was during that era of my life that I spent time in Phoenix. I was there for about six months on a job. As a traveling nurse, I spent time all over the country. I feel very fortunate that I've been able to see so many places.

I spent the last three years helping my friend Grace take care of her mother in her last years. When she lost her battle with dementia, Grace and I moved to Nashville to her mother's apartment here. It's been interesting, living in Nashville.

I'm cautiously optimistic about the man I'm dating. It started out as fake dating—long story—but we had our first "real" date the other night. That's when I hurt my foot. Hopefully, it's not an omen.

Update on my foot: it's still sore, but healing. I can finally take a shower without help, lol. I'm considering it a win!

Your curious daughter,

Breena

T HURSDAY MORNING, BREENA SAT in the steam-filled shower with water pounding down on her. The shower was her favorite place to think. And she had a lot to think about. The conversation with Laci yesterday about Gabe had stuck with her.

It had kept her awake, thinking about what Laci told her—that Gabe *didn't do relationships* and that she *shouldn't get her hopes up*. It had been like a glass of cold water in the face. She was fairly certain Laci hadn't meant to hurt her, but she really liked Gabe and thought he liked her back.

Her old insecurities about relationships were coming up, and she hated it. She turned off the water and grabbed the towel sitting on the toilet. Gingerly, Breena swung her legs out of the tub and onto the rug. This was the hard part—standing up one-legged without slipping and falling.

"Hey, I told you I'd help you." Laci rushed in from Breena's bedroom and steadied her.

Breena gave her a wry smile. "Sorry. I hate having to rely on others. I'm a horrible patient. Besides, I'm supposed to be taking care of you, not the other way around."

Laci laughed. "Well, it's time you let others help you, young lady. You've earned it."

Breena grinned and let Laci guide her out of the bathroom into her bedroom. "So how'd your meeting with Gabe go yesterday?"

"It was great. I'm really looking forward to the tour. It'll be fun to be on the road again, just like the old days when Gabe and I toured around."

"Oh, Gabe's going on tour with you?" Breena couldn't hide the surprise in her voice. "He didn't mention anything about that."

"Well, he's pretty careful about keeping his business and personal life separate, so I suppose it's not surprising he didn't say something."

Laci's offhand remark cracked Breena's already fragile confidence in their relationship. She lowered her head to hide the hurt.

"Would you like me to help you out to the living room?" Laci asked, unaware of the pain she'd inflicted.

"No, I think I'll stay in here and read," she said softly. The idea of having to be around Laci at that moment was unbearable

Breena opened her eyes and yawned; she must have dozed off. She found the book she'd been reading on the pillow next to her head. She could hear voices filtering into her room but wasn't sure where they were coming from. Listening a little longer, she identified Laci and Gabe. It sounded like they were in the kitchen or dining room.

Swinging her legs off the bed, she grabbed her crutches and stood up. Steadying herself before slowly moving, Breena looked forward to seeing Gabe again. She could smell something garlicky and wondered who had cooked.

As she made her way to the doorway, she stopped to steady herself before going into the dining room.

"It's going to be about three months in Asia. You good with being gone that long?" Gabe asked Laci.

"It's a long time, but it'll be good. What about you?"

"You know my priorities. I'm good too," he answered her.

Breena stopped. Three months? Gabe would be gone for three months? She remembered a similar conversation years ago.

Her mother had been talking with her new boyfriend. Breena hadn't meant to overhear. They'd been talking about a trip to California. Maeve said almost the same thing as Gabe. *I know my priorities. I'm good with this.* Initially, Breena thought she and her mother would be going to California. But the next day her mother dropped her off at school and never came back.

She caught a scent of pine—real or imaginary she wasn't sure—and was immediately transported to her mother's car with the cloying pine-scented air freshener. It was the last memory she had of her. She still couldn't stand the scent. It always brought back the feeling of being left. Of not being wanted. Of not being her mother's priority.

A wave of nausea hit hard. Breena reached for the doorway to keep from falling.

Chapter 22

GABRIEL

G ABRIEL WAS OUT OF his chair before he knew what was going on. He'd noticed Breena standing in her bedroom doorway, then all of a sudden, her face went pale and she started sliding toward the floor.

"Oh no you don't. Not again." He reached around her waist and steadied her as her crutches fell to the floor.

Laci gasped and rushed over to grab the crutches.

"I've got her, if you can get those," he said, nodding to the crutches. He reached under her knees and lifted her off the ground. *Just once, I'd like to carry her when she's conscious.*

He felt her startle as she came to. "Hey, hey. It's okay. I've got you." He wasn't sure where to go, so he carried her back into the bedroom and gently put her on the bed. He arranged the pillows behind her back, then stood aside as Laci came over with a cool wet cloth.

Laci looked almost as pale as Breena as she gently wiped Breena's face. "You scared the heck out of me, Bree." She took a deep breath. "What happened?"

Breena looked from Laci to Gabriel. "I guess...I tried too much too soon. Thank you for not letting me hit the ground." She gave him a little smile.

Her color was coming back, and Gabriel felt like he could breathe again. He was sure his heart stuttered when he saw her sliding down the doorframe.

"Can I get you anything?" he asked, feeling helpless.

She shook her head. "No...I'm starting to feel better."

"You feel like you could eat some soup? Mrs. Amati said you needed her soup, so she sent a large container for you."

Breena smiled, which was what he was hoping for. "Give me a minute and I'll be ready to eat."

He sat down on the bed next to her. "Mind if I wait with you?"

Laci moved to the doorway. "Would you like to eat in bed or in the dining room, Bree?"

"The dining room would be better. Just give me a few minutes."

"Okay, I'll get the table cleaned up and find a cushion for your foot." She headed out, leaving Gabriel alone with Breena.

He looked at her. Her head was leaned back, resting on a white pillowcase. Her hair, fanned out on the pillow, created a dark, red halo around her head. He picked up her hand and held it gently. "I think you may have taken a couple of years off my life."

She looked down at their hands. "Sorry. I...a wave of nausea hit me. I couldn't fight it off *and* keep my balance."

He tucked an errant hair behind her ear, his finger lingering a bit. It felt good to touch her. To be with her, even if they were in her bedroom only because she wasn't feeling well.

Breena skooched her legs off the edge of the bed. "Okay, I think I'm ready for Mrs. Amati's soup. That was what got me out of bed the first time. It smells so good."

"Hang on, let me help you." Gabriel walked around the bed to help her get her balance. "I can carry you, if it's easier." He waggled his eyebrows and received the desired response of a grin.

"You just want me in your arms."

"Guilty as charged," he said. "And just once, I'd like you awake while I'm carrying you."

Smiling, she said, "If you could get me one of my crutches, then I can lean on you for support."

"That's the best offer I've had today." He was happy the color had returned to her face, and her sense of humor was intact.

The next morning, Gabriel was having a hard time concentrating. Breena almost fainting last night had freaked him out. He hadn't even thought before he rushed over to keep her from hitting the floor; his legs acted on their own. In the microsecond before she started sliding, he'd seen her face go pale. He'd felt like his heart was pumping ice through his veins. He was grateful she'd perked up fairly quickly and eaten the soup. By the time he left, she looked much better, and it sounded like her ankle was feeling a little better too.

Ten minutes later, with no hope of getting anything done, he texted Breena.

GABRIEL: Hey, you up for a visitor?

BREENA: I just got dropped off at HV to visit your sister. Meet me here.

GABRIEL: OMW I'll give you a ride home later

The drive to his sister's assisted living facility was a pretty one. He pulled into the driveway, steering clear of an ambulance that had just pulled up.

He signed in and headed to Carly's room. His heart clenched when he realized he was following the EMTs. He walked into Carly's room just behind them; Breena sat next to Carly. An aide behind her was moving the breakfast tray away from the bed. The nurse came rushing in behind Gabriel with some files.

"What the heck is going on?" He tried to make his way to Carly.

Breena put up a finger to indicate he should hang on a second while she rattled off a bunch of stats to the EMTs. He heard her say she thought Carly's blood sugar level was dangerously low. The nurse who came in behind him was contradicting what Breena said.

But no one was telling Gabriel what was going on and that was frustrating.

"What's wrong with Carly?" He asked the nurse, who was now standing next to him.

"*She* called the ambulance and is trying to get them to take Carly to the hospital." The nurse pointed to Breena.

"What?" Gabriel looked back at Breena. "Breena, please let the nurse take over."

She looked up, and he could see the hurt in her eyes. "Gabe—"

"Breena, please leave Carly alone." Gabriel had finally made his way to his sister, who looked scared and reached for Gabriel's hand. "Let the professionals handle whatever is going on here."

Breena stumbled back a step, and the EMTs filled the space. One put a blood pressure cuff on Carly's arm, checked her eyes with a little flashlight, and felt her pulse, while the other asked the aide and nurse questions.

Gabriel still didn't have answers as to what had happened, but he held Carly's hand to keep them both calm. He talked softly to her while the EMTs did their job.

Minutes later, they brought in a gurney and strapped his sister on and wheeled her out of the room. Gabriel stood for a moment and looked around, only to find the room empty. This room that had, just seconds before, been noisy and chaotic was now eerily quiet. He rushed to the parking lot, jumped into his car, and followed the ambulance to the hospital, hoping to get some answers.

Chapter 23

BREENA

Dear Breena,

Do you mean to tell me that Maeve left you? When you were only nine years old? Who would do that to a child?!

I'm so sorry that happened.

I am forever grateful to the family who welcomed you. And to the investigator who was able to track me down.

It's confusing how life goes. Cindy and I wanted a family so desperately. She would have loved knowing you reached out to me.

We stopped trying to have a child when Cindy was diagnosed with cancer, five years after we were married. She fought it for so many years. We thought she'd beat it. We had ten years of cancer-free time together. But then it came back three years ago, and within six months, she was gone.

The last two and a half years have been hard. So thank you for reaching out and letting me know you exist. For letting me be part of your world, even if it's just via email. I treasure each letter I've gotten from you.

You're grateful father,

Peter

B REENA SAT ON THE bench outside Happy Valley, a tear running down her cheek. She'd been so stunned Gabe wouldn't listen to her. And when he told her to let the professionals handle it, she'd stumbled back and landed on her bad ankle.

With tears in her eyes, she hobbled her way, unnoticed, out of the room. She found the bench outside the front door and hoped to get a ride to the hospital with Gabe. But he'd rushed right past without even seeing her. At the time, she'd been too surprised to say anything, and now she had all kinds of things to say. Only problem was, he wasn't here to hear them.

She looked up to see Grace's small SUV pull up in front of her. Grace had responded to her text for a ride without question. Breena eased herself into the passenger seat, then sat staring at her hands. She appreciated Grace letting her ride in silence. Just having her best friend with her helped.

A few minutes later, Breena looked up as Grace pulled into another parking lot. She gave Grace a watery grin when she saw they were at an ice cream parlor a few blocks from their apartment. Ice cream had always been how they talked through things. It didn't seem to matter what the season or what the weather, ice cream solved all problems.

Grace helped her out of the car, and they walked into the 1950s-style ice cream parlor. You could sit at the counter or in one of the booths along the walls. They ordered their ice cream from the counter, then found an empty booth.

"Ready to talk?" Grace took a bite of her ice cream and closed her eyes. "Man, this is delicious." Grace had homemade cherry ice cream with chunks of Bing cherries throughout.

Settled in with a bowl of chocolate chip cookie dough in front of her, Breena took a spoonful, savoring the smooth flavors. She felt the sugar kick in and decided it was time to talk. "Yeah, I think so."

"Why did Gabriel leave you at Happy Valley?" Grace asked.

"He followed the ambulance to the hospital." At Grace's confused look, she added, "I think I need to start at the beginning."

So she told Grace about finding Carly unresponsive and what happened after that. The nurse had been no help. She'd argued with Breena, saying nothing was wrong, but the aide mentioned that Carly hadn't eaten in almost twenty-four hours. Carly had started to respond just before Gabe and the ambulance arrived. "When Gabe got there, he told me to get out of the way and let the professionals take care of Carly."

Grace looked up from her ice cream, a stunned look on her face. "He said that? He told you to get out of the way?"

"Yeah, he told me to leave Carly alone and let the professionals handle it. I'm sure walking in and seeing EMTs surrounding his sister had to have been really hard. And I know he doesn't like hospitals. He's made that clear. But..." Breena took a deep breath. "Not even listening to me? That really hurt."

"I can imagine." Grace took her time before asking the next question. "Why would he tell you to leave when you're the one who helped Carly?"

"The nurse told him I was making a big deal out of nothing, and it seems he believed her. Maybe he needed someone to lash out at and I was there?"

"Well, that's pretty crappy."

"It really is. I guess Laci was right. I'm not one of his priorities. No room in his life for me. Especially if he thinks I'm in the way."

"What are you saying?" Grace had a serious look on her face.

"I'm not sure. I can't be with someone if I'm not a priority for him. I sure as heck don't want to be with someone who sees no value in me. Who needs that?"

"Well, hopefully, he'll call soon with some sort of explanation," Grace offered.

Breena shrugged. She didn't want to talk about Gabe anymore. "So changing subjects. I've found my dad."

"What?" Grace's spoon paused midway to her mouth. "I...so the DNA test came back positive?"

Breena nodded as she took another bite.

"So tell me all about him. What's he like? And what the heck is his excuse for not being in your life?"

Breena grinned at Grace. Old friends were the best. "Well, his excuse is a pretty good one. He never knew I existed. I suppose I shouldn't be surprised Mom never told him. It sounds like they only went out for a few weeks, and when she left, he never heard from her again."

"Yep, that's a pretty good excuse." Grace grinned. "You sure he's actually your dad?"

"Yeah, the test was conclusive.."

"Wow. It sounds like the conversations are going well?" Grace asked.

It was weird having a conversation about her father. Especially a *good* conversation about him. It felt nice to have a family connection in the world beyond Grace.

"Yeah. It's going well." Breena grinned. "I never in my life expected to talk with my father, but I'm enjoying getting to know him. And the fact that he *wants* to know me is pretty amazing."

Breena's phone dinged again, signaling a text message.

"You going to check that?" Laci asked.

Breena and Grace had returned to the penthouse to find Laci making soup for dinner. She'd been getting text messages from Gabe all evening. In the first one, he'd apologized for the way he spoke to her at Happy Valley and wanted to make sure she'd gotten home okay. She didn't reply. After that, she hadn't even read the messages.

"No," Breena said, turning off the notifications for text messages.

"Has something happened?" Laci looked at her, confused. "You've been restless and silent since Grace brought you home. Speaking of, why did Grace bring you home? Where's Gabe?"

"He's at the hospital with Carly. Looks like he's on his phone if you want to text him."

With that, she stood up—a little shaky—and made her way to her bedroom. She really wanted to take a bath but wasn't completely sure she'd be able to get out when she was done. She wasn't in the mood to ask for help tonight, so she just lay in bed with her book.

Twenty minutes later, she heard a soft knock on her door. She sighed. Alone time was over.

"Come in," she called.

"I just talked to Gabe, and it sounds like Carly is doing well. They confirmed it was her blood sugar. They're keeping her overnight, but they feel like she'll be good to go back to the facility tomorrow," Laci told her. "I thought you'd like to know."

"Thank you. I'm glad to hear she'll be okay," Breena answered softly.

Laci walked in a little further. "Mind if I sit for a minute?"

Breena nodded and adjusted herself on the bed to make room.

"I realize it's none of my business, and you're welcome to tell me that, but what's going on? Gabe was concerned that you hadn't responded to his texts."

"I'm surprised he even noticed," she said bitterly.

Laci looked a little taken aback. "I know he's my friend, but so are you, Bree. What in the world did he do?"

"I suppose I should have listened to you. You were right. There's no room in his life for me."

"Listen, I probably shouldn't have said that. I'm sorry." Laci twisted her hands in her lap.

Breena shook her head. "No, you were right. He made that clear today."

"What do you mean?" Laci looked into Breena's eyes. "I just talked to him, and he sounded concerned about you."

Breena could see the confusion on Laci's face and told her the whole story of what happened.

"He told you to get away from Carly? And then he left you there? Crutches and all?" Laci sounded even more confused.

"He did. Listen, Laci, I respect you two have a long relationship, but I just don't need someone treating me like that in my life. I don't *want* that in my life. I want someone who wants me in *their* life and is willing to make me one of their priorities." She sighed.

"They all leave at some point, so I guess I should have expected this.."

"I can't believe he's messing with you like that. I'm really disappointed in him. If you'd like, I'll let him know to stop texting you." She took a deep breath. "And I'll move out if you want me to."

Breena gave her a watery smile and pulled her in for a hug. "You're not going anywhere until you're ready, Lace. I enjoy having you here. But I will take you up on your offer to tell him to stop texting me."

Dear Peter,

It sounds like we've both had some challenges over the years. I'm really sorry to hear about Cindy's battle with cancer.

I'm not sure what life would have looked like if we'd known about each other years ago. I'm grateful I grew up with Grace and her family. She's still my best friend, and I can't imagine my life without her.

I wish you lived closer. I'd love to have coffee with you, and a real conversation that I don't have to wait to get a response, lol.

Update on boyfriend: Turns out, he's a jerk and not worth my time and effort.

Update on foot: Getting there; I banged it around a bit today, which definitely didn't help.

Grateful to have a dad,

Breena

Chapter 24

GABRIEL

CRAP. GABRIEL WAS SITTING, again, in the hospital, scared he might lose someone important to him. Thankfully, Carly was alert and talking, which made this hospital visit much easier than when Breena had been here unconscious.

The room looked almost exactly like the one Breena had been in. Carly was covered with a warm blue blanket, and she seemed to be doing very well. Her color had improved since she'd gotten to the hospital.

She had an IV drip in her arm, and the doctor wanted to keep her overnight to make sure she was well hydrated. Breena had been correct about Carly's blood sugar being dangerously low.

He'd texted her several times, but she hadn't responded. He knew she'd read the first message, but it didn't look like she even saw any of the others.

Ding.

Laci: Breena requested that you not text her anymore

Gabriel: What? Why?

Laci: because she doesn't want to talk to you right now

Gabriel: can I call?

Laci: No. You screwed up, Gabe. Leave her alone for now.

Gabriel stared at his phone, hoping it would give him some answers. How had he screwed up?

"Gabe, you okay?" Carly broke into his thoughts.

He smiled at her. "As long as you're okay, I'm okay."

"But you look sad."

He didn't want to dump this on Carly. She probably wouldn't understand. It wasn't her problem; it was his. But she was the only person talking to him at the moment.

"I think I made Breena mad. But I'm not sure what I did."

"Probably when you told her to get away from me and didn't listen to her," Carly said matter-of-factly.

He looked at her, his heart stopping for a beat. "What did you say?"

"You told her to get away from me. It was a really dumb thing to say, Gabe, since it sounds like she's the one who saved me."

Oh crap. "I...I actually said that?"

"You told her to just leave me 'to the professionals.' I saw her face, Gabe. It turned kinda white. She almost fell down when she moved."

Gabriel dropped his face into his hands and let out a breath. He could feel a headache starting in his temples. No wonder she wasn't returning his texts and didn't want to hear from him.

"Carly, the aide said you didn't have dinner last night. Why didn't you eat?"

"The nurse said I was being bad because I don't like peas. She took my food away. I'm sorry I was bad, Gabe." She looked at him, a tear slowly tracking down her cheek. "I don't like when I'm bad."

Gabriel felt his temper rising, but he couldn't let it out on his sister. He wasn't mad at her. "Carly, you aren't a bad girl. I don't like peas either." He smiled.

He watched her eyes grow bigger. "You don't?"

"Nope. And I don't eat them either." He sat for a minute, holding her hand. "Is there anything else you don't like to do that they think is bad?"

"Well..." She looked down.

He knew she was concerned about making him mad, but that wouldn't happen. "It's okay, Carly. I'm not mad at you. And I won't be. I just need to know, okay?"

"Well, the one lady doesn't like it when I wake up early. Gina likes it when I wake up early. She helps me get dressed, and we sit and talk for a while, or I watch my TV. But the other lady won't let me get up and get dressed."

"Anything else?" It looked like he was going to have to do something different with Carly. He wasn't sure what though. He'd ask Breena. She'd have ideas.

He sighed when he remembered he couldn't ask her. He rubbed his chest, trying to relieve the ache.

Chapter 25

BREENA

Dear Breena,

I'm glad to hear your foot is getting better.

I'm sorry to hear things aren't going well with the boyfriend. Men can be really stupid sometimes. Keep that in mind. I hope you'll at least talk to him.

I'd love to have coffee with you as well. I've put my phone number at the bottom of the *email. Feel free to call anytime—with or without coffee.*

Sending you love,

Peter

T HE NEXT MORNING BREENA slammed open the door to Gabe's office. He looked up, startled. She'd tried to cool her head on the drive over, but everything was still too fresh. She hadn't gotten any sleep last night, which definitely didn't help her disposition.

She stood in front of his desk, hands on her hips, staring. He looked like he'd had a similar night. Laci mentioned he'd gone into the office to respond to a few emails this morning, so Breena decided this was the time to face him.

He silently stood up behind his desk.

"Nothing to say?" she asked. "All those texts you sent, and now you have nothing to say?"

"I'm sorry." His voice came out gravelly, reminding her he'd probably spent the night at the hospital with Carly.

Breena stood for a moment staring at him. "Is that all?"

"I...I'm not sure what else there is to say. I'm so sorry, Breena."

"Well, I have something to say." She walked a little closer to his desk, her eyes narrow. "What exactly are you sorry for, Gabe? Sorry you didn't take me to the hospital with you? Sorry you left me stranded at Happy Valley to find a ride for myself? Sorry you insulted my nursing skills? Sorry you trusted the word of the nurse over mine?"

She could see his eyes grow wider with each question. He fell back into his chair and looked up at her. He opened his mouth to speak, but she wasn't done.

"I won't be with someone who doesn't value me, Gabe."

"I—"

"And I most certainly won't be with someone who doesn't trust me."

"I—" He tried to speak again, but she still wasn't done.

"You told me when we first met, you had no interest in dating and you had no room in your life for anyone other than your sister and your clients. I obviously should have believed you, so that one's on me."

"Breena, please—"

"Please what, Gabe?" When he didn't respond, she turned on her heel and walked back to the door. "Don't bother calling, Gabe. We're done."

She   turned   on   her   heel   and walked—limped—out.

Dear Peter,

Well, I've broken up with Gabe. The sad thing is, we only had one date. We've been going out for two weeks, but only had one <u>real</u> date.

I'm sad about how this ended. I really liked him. But like you said, men are stupid. At least Gabe is.

I'll write soon, but for tonight, I'm going to have a good cry.

Your sad daughter,

Breena

Dear Breena,

I'm sorry about your breakup. I hope you had a good cry. When you're ready to talk, just let me know.

Always here for you,

Peter

Breena rolled over in bed, annoyed it was already morning. Annoyed she'd wasted the last week moping in bed. Annoyed her friends were starting to get concerned. She knew it was time to give them a break.

Today was the day to start mixing with people again. *Ugh.* She didn't feel like peopling today but knew it was important for Laci and Grace to see her up and about. And her ankle needed to move.

Pushing herself out of bed, she looked at the tulips on her nightstand. Gabe had sent them after she broke up with him. They were starting to droop. She picked up the card and read it for the hundredth time. *I'm so sorry I didn't have enough trust in you. Please call me.*

She held the card to her heart as she took a moment to see how her ankle felt. She moved it around in all directions, put a little weight on it, and determined it was time to try to shower standing up. Just the thought brought a small smile to her face. She looked back down at the card in her hand. Today might be the day. *We'll see.*

She peeked out her window just in time to see the sun making its appearance on the horizon. The sky was stunning. It was the beginning of February, and she knew it was still cold out, but all of a sudden she wanted to go into the world. With one last glance at the horizon, she headed to the bathroom.

It felt so good to *stand* under hot pulsing water again. She appreciated the help Laci and Grace had given her over the past week and a half, but man, was it nice to do it by herself.

Forty-five minutes later, showered, dressed, and in a better mood, Breena made her way to the kitchen. The rest of the apartment was still quiet, so she made a pot of coffee and decided it was time to bake again. She looked at the dozen pink roses on the kitchen counter. They had come the second day. The card, tucked away in her drawer, had been simple. *I'm so sorry I acted like an idiot! I hope you can forgive me*

She moved the flowers to the dining room table so she had counter space to bake.

On the third day, Gabe sent a dozen orange roses. Their card had simply said, *I miss you.* Those roses were in the living room.

The violet roses were from day four, and the card had a heart with its message. *Carly misses you too.* That had been a bit of a low blow, in her opinion. She missed CeeCee too. She'd desperately wanted to visit her in the hospital to make sure she was okay, but she didn't want to run into Gabe. That vase was on the turquoise table in the entryway.

Yesterday, a dozen white roses showed up. They were, as all the flower arrangements were, stunning. The card on that one read, *My heart misses your heart.*

Today, she decided it was time to deal with Gabe and all of his beautiful flowers. She'd realized Gabe was the only man who'd ever made his way into her heart, and she wasn't ready to walk away. But she needed to find out if it was real. And if he was serious.

First, though, she was going to do some baking. It felt good to be back in the kitchen. She hadn't realized how much she missed it. She gathered the ingredients for a French toast casserole that was everyone's favorite. After putting it in the oven, she sat at the dining room table, staring at the pink flowers, to enjoy a cup of coffee while it baked. When there were only fifteen minutes left on the timer, she got up again and prepped some bacon.

Within minutes of putting the bacon in the oven, the whole house smelled like breakfast. Knowing the scent would bring hungry women soon, she pulled out a couple of coffee cups and set the table.

Laci was the first to come out. "Oh my gosh. What is that incredible smell?"

Breena saw her do a small double take when she saw Breena in the kitchen, fully dressed, hair done, baking again. But instead of saying anything, Laci just came over and gave her a big hug.

"Man, I'm going to miss you when you go home." Breena sighed and leaned into the hug.

"I'm going to miss you too. And I'm really going to miss your cooking." Laci grinned at her. "What's in the oven that smells so good?"

Grace came plodding through the dining room doorway from the living room. "I smell bacon. Please tell me it's bacon. Oh, Bree! I'm so happy to see you up and about." Grace came around the island and gave Breena another big hug.

The arrival of Jillian via the elevator completed her group. She'd texted Jilly to see if she was available for breakfast with them and was glad she could join them. After a hug from Jillian, her world felt whole again.

Well, mostly.

"Ladies, thank you for taking good care of me over the past week, but I've decided it's time to get back into life." Breena smiled at each of them, then turned to pull everything from the oven. "I just realized how much I've missed being in the kitchen. Now go have a seat. I'll bring everything over in a minute."

Breakfast with friends was exactly what she needed, Breena realized. Not just nutritionally, but she'd been hiding in her room and really missed them.

"So tell me what I've missed. What's going on with the tour?" she asked Laci.

"It's coming together so well. I can't believe it's almost here. The first few weeks are here in the US. Kind of a pretour, if you will. We're leaving next week to get it started."

"Oh..." Breena paused for a moment. "I didn't realize you were leaving so soon."

"I'm playing at the Opry in two days. You have to come. I have tickets for you, Grace and Carl, and Jilly."

Breena wasn't sure what to say. She wanted to see Laci perform at the Opry, but she wasn't sure how things were going with Gabe.

"I won't take no for an answer." Laci seemed to read her mind.

Breena grinned at her. "I can't wait to see you at the Opry. It's going to be amazing."

"It'll be my first time in public in any meaningful way," Laci said softly. She looked a little nervous.

Grace and Breena each put a hand on Laci's.

"It's going to be great. Don't let anything or any-one ruin the night for you," Grace said.

Breena smiled at that and gave Laci's hand a little squeeze. "It will be your night to shine. Everyone will love you."

Jillian spoke for the first time. "I have an idea. How about if we all go out tonight? Since Bree can't dance, let's do karaoke. We can resurrect Leather and Laci...maybe with a little less leather though."

"Ooh, that would be fun," Grace piped up.

"Do I get to go in a wig?" Laci asked.

"You can go however you want," Jillian said.

They all turned to Breena, who hadn't said any-thing yet.

Grace reached over and took her hand. "You in?"

Breena nodded. "Yeah, I'm in." Maybe a night out with her friends was what she needed right now.

Dear Peter,

Thank you for your patience. I'm headed out tonight but would love to call tomorrow morning to chat over coffee. I hope the timing works for you. I'll shoot you a text before I call, just to make sure.

Looking forward to talking,

Breena

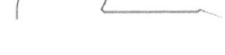

Later that evening, the women gathered in the living room, waiting for their ride to pick them up for their night out. Breena looked at her friends, excited to go out with them.

Laci had opted to go incognito and wore the brown pixie-cut wig again with jeans, boots, and a purple flannel shirt. The rest of them decided not to wear wigs for the evening. Breena wore some black cowboy boots with her jeans and a black tank top under her denim jacket. Jillian was the only one who had opted to wear a dress with her cowboy boots.

Later, Breena was settled on a stool at the bar, watching her friends on stage. Jillian, it turned out, was a karaoke queen. She talked Laci into joining her, and they settled on a Dolly Parton song.

Grace sat on the stool beside her, her fringe swaying as she picked up her beer.

"I love seeing you in colorful clothes," Breena said, looking at Grace's turquoise boots, yellow jeans, and white pearl-snap shirt with yellow fringe.

"Yeah, it took me a little bit to remember I love wearing color." She smiled at Breena.

They sat back and enjoyed listening to their friends singing Dolly's "I Will Always Love You." It amazed Breena, again, just how beautiful Jillian's voice was.

And her voice mixed with Laci's was exquisite.

"Man, I'd love for the two of them to sing at our wedding," Grace said.

Breena looked at her. "That would be amazing, wouldn't it?"

A few minutes later, Laci and Jillian rejoined them, at the ready for a couple of drinks.

"Jilly, the bartender at the far end of the bar seems to be pretty quick. Maybe you should wander that way to get the drinks," Grace said with a mischievous grin on her face.

"Oh, thanks, Grace." Jillian headed off in search of liquid sustenance.

"What're you up to?" Breena asked, looking at her.

Grace giggled. "You'll never guess who I saw over there on my way back from the restroom." At their questioning looks, she continued, "Tex! Remember him from our first night out dancing?"

"Oh my gosh." Breena started laughing.

"Wait, who's Tex?" Laci asked. "How come I haven't heard of him before?"

"We're not sure what his real name is, but he was sweet and thought he helped Jilly out of a bind."

Several minutes later, Jillian came back with two drinks and a big smile on her face. "You'll never guess who I just ran into," she said, a little out of breath.

"Who?" The faux-innocence on their faces must have given them away.

Jillian started laughing. "You knew he was over there, didn't you, Grace?"

"Guilty as charged." She laughed.

"Well, thank you." She grinned. "He's still sexy as all get out." She waggled her brows and took a deep drink of beer. "Okay, girls, let's make this our last round then head home.."

Breena laughed as they finished their drinks and secured a taxi. It was always good medicine, hanging out with friends.

Chapter 26

GABRIEL

SITTING AT THE BREAKFAST table with Carly and Gina, Gabriel realized just how much had changed in the past week. Some good and some...well, he missed Breena.

"So what color today?" he asked Carly, who was finishing up her cereal. Gabriel sipped his coffee while he waited.

"I think yellow," Carly answered, her spoon stopping halfway to her mouth. "I asked Gina to help me, and we looked them up online and yellow is a good color to say *I'm sorry* with."

"Well, that sounds perfect then." Gabe nodded. "I'll order yellow flowers on my way to the office."

He got up and put his cup in the dishwasher, then turned back to Carly and Gina. "Are you sure you two will be okay?" He asked every single time he left them, but he still wasn't used to the huge responsibility of having Carly live with him.

"We'll be just fine, *Mommy*," Carly said in a playful voice.

He swatted at her, making her laugh, then pulled her in for a hug. "I'm glad you're here, Goof." He smiled into her hair, his heart feeling full, as it always did when he gave her a hug. Some people probably thought Carly was a burden, but there wasn't a single day he'd felt that way. And now that she was living under his roof...well, he was happy. They were still working out the bumps of how to live together, but they were getting there.

Gabriel reluctantly headed back to his newly created home office, trying to figure out what he needed to take to the downtown office that morning. The first few days after Carly and Gina moved in, he'd worked only from home to make himself available to them. It was weird and hard having others in his home after living alone for so long.

Having Carly around was mostly a good distraction for his hurting heart. A few times she'd asked if Breena could visit her at her new home, but there'd been no communication between them since she'd left his office. He had no idea if she wanted to visit Carly or not.

Grabbing his briefcase, he headed back into the living room and said goodbye to Carly and Gina. "Have fun, don't make a huge mess, I left some soup and stuff for sandwiches for lunch, and don't burn down the house."

Carly giggled and hugged him. "See ya later, alligator." She called as he headed out the door.

"See ya soon, raccoon.," he responded, looking back over his shoulder with a smile.

It was a short trip to the best florist in town, and he'd been giving her a lot of business the past several days. The bell over the door jingled as he stepped inside, enjoying the overload to his senses. "Good morning, Mrs. Snowden."

"My goodness, Gabriel. More flowers? What in the world did you do to your girl?" Mrs. Snowden grinned at him.

"Still hoping she'll forgive me for being really stupid ," Gabriel said wryly.

"Are we doing roses again? What color?" she asked at his nod.

"I think yellow today, if you have them."

"I just got a delivery of gorgeous yellow roses yesterday, so that's perfect." She busied herself, grabbing a vase and some greenery.

"Actually, can you do two different yellow arrangements today?" he asked.

"Don't tell me you done ticked off two women, Gabriel." She gave him a stern look, her hands on her ample hips.

He laughed. "No, I can't keep up with one woman. I was thinking of sending the second arrangement to my sister. She helped me pick out the color today, and I know yellow is her favorite."

Fifteen minutes later, he was walking out of an elevator and into his office.

"Good morning, Mr. van Neugh," Kelly greeted him.

"Morning, Kelly. When you have a few minutes, I'd like to speak with you in my office."

"Of course, sir. Would you like a coffee?" She stood as he walked past her desk, ready to follow him.

"Only if you're getting one for yourself. Otherwise, I'll grab one later." Gabriel turned and almost bumped into her.

"Sorry, sir." She backed up a step. "I'll go grab our coffees." She hurried off to the small kitchenette.

Gabriel had a proposal for Kelly and wasn't at all sure how it was going to go over. She seemed so skittish and uncertain so often, but she was excellent at her job and remembered everything she worked on. She would need both of those skills for the idea he had in mind.

He sat behind his desk and rubbed his hands over his face. It had been a long couple of weeks, and he hadn't slept well since Carly had been in the hospital and Breena broke up with him.

"You okay, sir?" Kelly had stopped in the doorway and was looking at him.

"Yeah, just tired. Come on in, Kelly, and take a seat. And thanks." He took the coffee from her and enjoyed the jolt to his system that came with the first sip.

"I have a proposal for you and hope this is something you might be open to," Gabriel started.

Her eyes went wide, full of concern. "A...proposal, sir?"

"I've never asked about your personal life, because it's none of my business, but—"

"I...sir?" She looked terrified by what she thought he was proposing.

Gabriel stopped.. "No, no. Nothing unsavory, Kelly. I promise." He waited a beat for her to relax. "I was wondering if you would be open to travel?"

"You want me to travel, sir?"

"Well, with the tour starting... Let me start from the beginning. This might be too much information, but it's important to the conversation."

He watched her shoulders relax, and she nodded.

"Okay, you know the US part of the tour is starting next week. Laci will be gone for three weeks, visiting different venues around the country."

"Right." She could probably list every date and venue without notes.

"We hire a tour manager to handle most of the details, but normally, I'd go along for the first few stops to make sure nothing goes wrong. But I can't do that this time. My younger sister and her caretaker just moved in with me, and I need to hire a partner to help with all the business." He took another sip of coffee.

"So I was hoping you might be willing to step in as tour manager for this leg of the tour."

"You want me to travel with Laci and the bands for three weeks? I'm not a tour manager."

He could see her thinking about it, which gave him hope. "No, you're not. Although I think you'd be exceptional at it. You know every single detail of this tour. There is already a tour manager in place, but I want you handling the performers. You would have an assistant to help with running around and details. There would, of course, be a bump in pay to go along with the new job responsibilities."

"But I'm not at all qualified, sir."

"Why don't you think about it, then let me know what you think?"

She gave a quick nod, stood up, and walked slowly back to her desk.

Twenty minutes later, a light tap on his door told him his next potential big change was here. He felt like this meeting might go similarly to the one with Kelly. But he knew Kelly was the right person for that job, and Jackson was the right person for this next proposal.

"Hey, Jackson, come on in." Gabriel stood up and met him at the front of the desk, where they shook hands.

"Gabriel, good to see you."

"Let's go into the conference room, if you don't mind. I left all the papers for us in there." At Jackson's nod, he led the way out of his office to the conference room. He noticed Kelly had already set up fresh coffee and some fruit. Man he was going to miss her if she took him up on his offer. He walked over to grab a cup of coffee and several apple slices, then took a seat at the table.

Jackson took a seat at the head of the table adjacent to Gabriel and set his coffee and fruit down. "So what's on your mind, Gabriel? You've got my curiosity piqued." He smiled, then took a drink of his coffee. "This is good stuff."

Gabriel smiled back. "It is, and I'm going to miss it if Kelly takes me up on the offer I made her today. I'm just going to be straight and tell you what I want. My business is doing really well, but it leaves no room for any kind of a personal life. And for the first time in my career, I'd like some margins. So I'd like to offer you the opportunity to be my business partner."

He watched Jackson's eyes go wide. "Wow, that is not what I was expecting. At all." He laughed a little.

Gabriel grinned. "What'd you think I called you for?"

"Well, to be honest, I thought it'd be about some young performer you wanted or something like that. Which actually, I saw someone I'd like to talk about. Sometimes listening to karaoke is painful, but last night there were some gems." He chuckled. "But I have to say, this is a very interesting offer. Tell me more."

Jackson Starr was Ms. Tessa Starr's grandson, and he helped her cull the best of the new musicians they came across. Gabriel knew he had a good ear for musicians and a smart mind for the business. He also knew Jackson was fair and honest, which wasn't a guarantee in this industry.

They talked for the next two hours as Gabriel laid out his vision for the business and his life. With the coffee carafe empty and the fruit tray picked over, they decided to head to lunch down the block.

Going back to the office after lunch, Gabriel was pleased with how his time with Jackson had gone. He knew whatever decision Jackson made regarding his offer would be a thoughtful one. But he hoped Jackson would take him up on it. Just like he hoped Kelly would take him up on the proposal he'd made her, even though it would leave a hole in the office that would need to be filled.

"Mr. van Neugh, do you have a minute?" Kelly caught him as soon as he walked in the door.

"Of course. Come on in, Kelly." He headed into his office and left the door open for her to follow. He seated himself in one of the two chairs in front of his desk and turned it to face the other. She stood for a second, twisting her hands together before seeming to make a decision and sitting down. Gabriel waited patiently for her to tell him whatever she needed to talk about.

"First off, I want to say thank you for the offer. It sounds exciting. Second, I think I need to share a bit of my own story with you, since you were open with me." Her hands fidgeted in her lap before she folded them together. "Do you mind if I close the door?"

Gabriel nodded. "Feel free to lock the front door if you want. Whatever makes you comfortable." He waited while she went to the main door and locked it. Then she closed the door to his office on her way back in.

She blew out a big breath. "My story isn't very long or exciting, but..." She steadied herself. "I'm recently divorced from a man who was...not very nice. I moved to Nashville, hoping to start a new life, but he keeps calling me and won't leave me alone."

Gabriel felt his eyebrows go up, but he didn't say anything.

"I've filed for a restraining order, but I don't know if it will make him stop calling me. So yes, I would like to take you up on the travel. But I need a small advance to buy a new phone and change apartments. I know this is more than you probably bargained for, but I thought you should know before I agreed to your offer."

"Thank you, Kelly, for sharing that with me. That has to make for an unsettling experience at home. Do you have anywhere to stay if you move out of your apartment?" With Laci's recent history and the safe space in Breena's apartment in mind, Gabriel was willing to do what was needed to help Kelly.

She looked down at her hands, fidgeting again in her lap. "I guess it depends on how quickly I can find a new apartment."

"Well, the thing is, I happen to know a space that might be available for you. If you're interested, I can ask and see if it's open at the moment."

Kelly nodded her head slightly. "Yes, I...I would like that. Thank you, Mr. van Neugh."

"Kelly." He sighed. "I'd really like it if you called me Gabriel."

She looked up with wide eyes, then gave him a small smile. "I'll try, sir. Gabriel."

At the knock on the office door, she headed out and closed his door behind her. Gabriel smiled and shook his head. It had been a fruitful day. Two very big changes, but both would free up time and space in his life. Time and space he hoped to convince Breena to fill.

He looked up at the tap on his door. Kelly poked her head in. "Got a delivery here for you, sir." She stepped back, and Breena came in with a vase full of roses in a variety of colors. Kelly smiled and backed out of the door. "I'm heading out for the day, sir."

He nodded absently at Kelly as he watched Breena step up to the desk and set the vase in the middle, on top of a pile of papers. She looked amazing. But it wasn't the jeans or oatmeal colored sweater that caught his attention; it was her energy that always drew him in. She was a beautiful person inside and out. His heart was beating double-time anticipating what she had to say..

Before he could say anything, she spoke. "This one"—she pointed to the bright green rose in the middle of the vase—"means good news." The right side of her lips quirked up. "And this one"—she pointed to the yellow rose—"means forgiveness." She looked at him with an eyebrow raised, then back down at the roses, pointing to the light pink flower. "And this one, means appreciation."

He felt his lips turn down, but she continued.

"I want you to know that I appreciate a man who can apologize."

He grinned at that.

She pointed to the burgundy rose. "This one means devotion. Your devotion to your sister is one of your finest qualities."

He was having a hard time staying seated, but she seemed to be on a mission and he needed to let her finish. Besides, he wanted to hear what else she had to say.

She was pointing now to the deep blue rose near the center. "This one means mystery. And this orange one means fascination. You are a huge mystery to me, Gabe. One I think will be fascinating to figure out. I think mystery in a relationship is important. To some extent."

Her eyes twinkled as she looked down at him. She looked back at the vase. "This one"—she pointed to the cream-colored rose—"means thoughtfulness, and the peach one means gratitude. The women of the penthouse appreciate your thoughtfulness for sending so many lovely roses. We have all been enjoying them, so thank you." She grinned at him again. "And I have a lot of gratitude for the notes you sent with them. Again, a man who can say I'm sorry and forgive me in writing is someone I'm glad to know."

He couldn't take his eyes off her. He would accept gratitude and appreciation if that was all she had for him. He looked at her and wondered when, exactly, he had fallen in love with her. He wasn't sure, but he most certainly had done so somewhere along the way. The thought should have scared him, but instead, it brought him peace. His whole body relaxed into the emotion.

"You okay?" She was looking at him through narrow eyes.

"Yeah, I'm very much okay." He smiled.

"I've got two more for you. This yellow one with red on the edges, it means happiness. While granted, I haven't been super happy with you this past week, I do know you have the capacity to make me happy, to make my heart happy."

He saw her take a deep breath; it seemed to be a little shaky which made him wonder what the lavender flower meant.

"And this last flower…" She plucked it out of the vase and handed it to him. "Do you know what a lavender rose means?"

He shook his head and looked at the blossom in his hand.

"Look it up." She smiled down at him. "I'll see you tomorrow night at the Opry." She turned and headed out the door.

He watched her walk out, completely confused as to what he should do next. He wanted to rush after her, but it seemed she wanted him to figure out what the light purple rose meant first.

"Kelly," he hollered, then remembered she'd left when Breena came in.

"Nope, just me." Jackson stuck his head in.

"Oh, hey, Jackson. Any idea what the meaning of a lavender rose is?"

"Roses have meanings?"

Gabriel laughed. "Never mind. I'll stop and ask Mrs. Snowden on the way home. Anyway, what can I do for you?"

Chapter 27

BREENA

Dear Peter,

It was so great talking to you yesterday. I have a lot to catch you up on, even though it's only been a day since we spoke.

Update on my foot: so, so much better. I'm able to walk without a crutch, which is nice

Update with Gabe: After a week of receiving flowers every single day, I decided it was time to talk with him. I have forgiven him and gave him a few flowers of my own ;)

I'm headed to the Grand Ole Opry tonight to watch a friend perform. I can't wait!

I'll share more tomorrow.

Love,

Breena

SITTING FRONT ROW OF the Grand Ole Opry on a Friday night was quite the experience. Breena looked around the beautiful theater as they waited for the show to begin. The pew-like benches behind them gave the theater a bit of a church feel, the red cushions standing out.

To Breena's left, Grace, in her turquoise cowboy boots and jeans, was grinning at Carl and pointing to the stage. They looked like they were reliving a happy memory. One of their first dates had been to the Grand Ole Opry.

On her other side, Jillian was decked out in yellow cowboy boots, black tights, jean-shorts, and a yellow top that matched her boots. Jillian looked a little more dolled up than she or Grace did, which made Breena wonder.

Breena wore her red cowboy boots with a pair of jeans and a red leather vest over a white T-shirt.

The lights went down and the show began. The host for the evening welcomed the sold-out crowd and told everyone there was a special guest joining them at the end of the show. Breena could feel a buzz of energy in the theater.

After the other musical guests were finished, it was time for Laci.

"Ladies and gentlemen, who's ready for the surprise guest we have for you tonight?"

The theater roared with claps and shouts.

"I think y'all are going to love this one. Actually, I know you will. Three-time country music artist of the year and a favorite here at the Opry, help me welcome Laci Love."

The audience went wild as Laci walked onto the stage. She greeted the house band on her way past and gave the host a hug before walking up to the microphone in the golden circle center stage.

"Hey, y'all. How's everyone doin' tonight?"

Breena watched as Laci grinned down directly at them with a little wink before she looked at the crowd.

"It's been a minute since I've been here. Thank y'all for the warm welcome back. You know, this is one of my favorite places to perform. I'm getting ready to head out on the road for several months, but I wanted to kick things off here. Tonight. With y'all."

Breena enjoyed watching Laci work the crowd. She'd gotten to know Laci the past few weeks, but other than the time at Laci's house when they'd pretended to be a band and then at the karaoke bar, she'd never seen her in her element—on stage.

Laci went through the first song, her first number-one hit, "Love Letter to You." It was a sweet song with a fun chorus and at least half the audience sang along with her. Even though Breena didn't know a lot of country music, she did know that one.

"Now I've got some special friends here tonight, and I'd like to call one of them up on stage with me. Jillian, will you come on up here and help me with this next song?"

Breena looked over at Jillian, stunned. But Jillian smiled at Breena before she jumped up and headed for the stage.

They sang the song they'd performed in Laci's home studio. It sounded even better than the first time. Breena wondered if they'd practiced at some point. Their voices harmonized together so perfectly.

At the end of the song, Jillian gave Laci a hug, graciously accepted the applause, and headed off stage. Breena watched as a tall man met her in the corridor. They talked for a minute, then Jillian came back to her seat, her face flushed.

"Oh my gosh, that was amazing, Jilly." Breena hugged her. Carl and Grace leaned over to offer their own compliments and congratulations.

Jillian was beaming. "Thanks. It was so hard to keep it a secret from you, but Laci really wanted it to be a surprise."

"Well, it definitely was." Breena grinned. "Hey, who was that man talking with you backstage?"

Color crept up Jillian's face again. "It was Tex. He said he was planning on texting me next week. He wants to run an idea by me."

Breena grinned at the fact that Tex kept popping up for Jillian. "Oh my gosh. What was he doing back there?"

"I'm not really sure. He congratulated me on a great performance. I was too surprised at seeing him to ask any questions. But, dang gurl, he looked good." She laughed.

As the show wrapped up, they filed toward the back of the theater with the rest of the audience. Before they got very far, Breena noticed Ms. Tessa Starr moving toward them against the flow of people.

She gave Breena a smile and *a lovely to see you, darling*. She smiled at Grace, tilted her head to the side with a curious look on her face, then turned to Jillian. "Darling, that was a wonderful performance."

"Oh, thank you," Jillian said.

"I'm Tessa Starr." She paused and Breena heard Grace gasp. "I know a thing or two about country music and what it takes to make it in this town." She handed Jillian a card. "You need to come to my house next month for our next gathering. The date is on the back of the card."

She turned to leave, but Grace spoke up. "Ms. Starr." She caught the woman's attention.

"Yes, dear?"

"I think you knew my mother, Marilyn Parson...well, probably Marilyn Carlisle then."

Ms. Starr froze and stared at Grace. "You're Marilyn's girl? You're little Dolly?"

Grace grinned. "Well, I go by Grace now, but yes." She stuck one of her booted feet out. "I just learned you bought my mom these boots."

Ms. Starr looked at the turquoise boot then back up to Grace's face, her eyes glittering with unshed tears, but a smile across her lips. "Oh my stars, she loved those boots. Your mama always had the best shoes."

She reached over and hugged Grace. "Marilyn was a treasure. I was so sorry to hear she passed away." She paused, her focus on Grace for a moment longer. "I'll see you again soon," she said to Jillian before she walked back up the aisle.

Grace looked at Breena. "I see what you mean. Wow. She's a force of nature."

Gabriel came up behind them and tapped Breena on the shoulder. "Breena, may I borrow you for a few minutes please?"

She'd missed his low voice and the effect it had on her stomach.

She glanced at Grace, who raised an eyebrow. She'd told Breena and Laci what she'd done the previous day, and they were all waiting to hear Gabe's response. She gave Grace a slight nod and followed Gabe backstage. They wound their way through musicians, stagehands, and others hanging out. Breena wasn't sure where they were going.

He finally slowed down when they came to the dressing rooms and pulled her into one with a Honky Tonk Angels placard on the door. Laci was sitting at one end of the room, where the whole wall was mirror and lights. She looked up when they walked in.

Breena rushed over to her. "Oh my gosh, Laci. What a great show! Thank you so much for getting us tickets to see you tonight and for having Jillian sing with you."

"I'm so glad you all came. It was like having my family in the front row. And it was so much fun to have Jilly come up on stage with me." Laci smiled at her.

"Lace, can I boot you out for a couple of minutes, please?" Gabe interrupted.

Confused, she stood and gathered a few things. "Sure, no problem." She headed out the door, closing it behind her.

Gabe walked to Breena, who had stopped in the middle of the room. His face was unreadable.

"What's going on Gabe?"

"Two things. First, do you have space at your place for a guest?"

Completely thrown off and more than a little disappointed for the reason he'd pulled her in here, Breena took a second to gather her thoughts. "Um, yes. It's empty right now. Why?"

"Kelly, my secretary, needs a safe space for the next few days, and I was wondering if she could stay there."

"Oh. Yeah, sure. No problem. Just let me know when, and we'll be ready for her."

"Tomorrow midmorning if that works for you. I'd like to get her out of her place as soon as possible."

Breena nodded. "Bring her over anytime. I'll let Brian know to expect you."

"Thank you. I really appreciate that." He walked around the dressing room, then stopped in front of her, his hands behind his back. "Lavender roses mean love at first sight."

The grin came slowly to her face. "Yes, it does."

"Do you know what red roses mean?" he asked, his eyes staring intently into hers.

Her pulse ramped up. "I'm pretty sure they mean love."

He pulled his hand from behind his back. He had a red rose. He held it out to her. "Yes, it does."

She took the rose and noticed her hands were shaky. He took a step closer, the tips of their boots touching. He reached up and ran his fingers down her cheek. "God, you're beautiful. I've missed you."

And he wrapped his arms around her.

Breena took a deep breath, relaxing against his body, and looked up at his handsome face. "So you know you actually have to say it for it to count, right?"

He leaned back just enough to look down at her. "What?"

She held up the red rose. "You have to say it."

He grinned, leaning down until his lips were a breath away from hers. "Oh, do I? Well, Ms. Breena O'Malley, I love you." He closed the space between their lips, sighing.

Breena's body buzzed with anticipation when his lips finally touched hers. Without thinking, she put her arms around his neck, her fingers absently playing with his hair.

She pulled back slightly to look up into his eyes and grinned. "Well, that's awfully convenient, Mr. van Neugh, because I love you too." She stretched up and fitted her lips to his again. It might be a mistake to love Gabriel van Neugh, but Breena couldn't help how her heart felt.

Chapter 28

GABRIEL

A WEEK LATER, GABRIEL sat in the dining room of the safe apartment with Laci and Kelly, papers covering the whole table. He was finishing up going over all the final details with both women.

"This looks good, ladies." He looked up from the stack of papers in front of him. "Kelly, I think you're going to be brilliant in your new position. You're already a huge asset to the team."

Kelly blushed at the compliment. "Thank you for this opportunity, sir...um, Gabriel. I'm really enjoying it so far. And Laci has been a huge help making sure I understand everything."

Laci studied him for a moment. "You're never this relaxed and calm before a tour. What's going on?"

Gabriel grinned at Kelly. "She's at least part of the reason. Knowing I don't have to get on that bus tomorrow morning is a relief. And knowing it will go smoothly, even when I'm not there—that's amazing."

Laci smiled, then pushed her chair back. "I'm looking forward to having her on the road too. If we're done here, I've got to take off."

"Laci, you headed to band practice?" Gabriel asked.

"Actually off to wardrobe for some final fittings and design approvals." She brushed a hand along Kelly's shoulder as she walked past. "You let me know if you need anything, Kelly. See you two later." She headed to the other side, through the secret sliding door.

"I have a new cell phone for you." Gabriel set the phone on the table and slid it across to her. "I hope this will help with your ex not being able to reach you."

"Oh." Kelly looked at the phone. "Thank you. I planned to get one when I return."

Gabriel brushed it off. "No problem. I've put my number in and Laci's. Be careful who else you give the new number to."

She nodded.

"I know it's going to be a challenge to get yourself organized to leave along with your new responsibilities. Grace has offered to help get whatever you need for the tour."

Just then, Grace poked her head in. "Okay for me to come in?"

"Come on in, Grace. I was just talking about you." Gabriel grinned at her. The women of the penthouse had become a small family, and they welcomed Kelly in right away. Gabriel had seen a difference already in the few hours she'd been here. These women were good for her. "I'm going to head out and work from home for the rest of the day. You ladies have fun with your shopping."

Gabriel went through the sliding panel, hoping to catch Breena before going home, but he was disappointed to find she was gone.

Walking into his townhouse, the first thing Gabriel noticed was that it smelled like heaven. Something spicy, garlicky, tomatoey. He immediately thought of Breena as his stomach growled. He walked further into the house and could hear laughing female voices from the direction of the kitchen. After dumping his briefcase and jacket in his office, he headed back to see what was going on.

Stepping into dining room-kitchen combo, he saw Gina, Carly and Breena sitting at the table. He couldn't stop the smile, nor did he want to. Gabriel stood in the doorway and stared for a moment, unobserved by the women. Coming home to find Breena here felt so right. And because he now had a partner, he would come home at a reasonable hour on a regular basis.

"Well, look at this table full of beautiful women," he commented as he walked into the room.

"Gabe!" Carly jumped out of her chair to hug him.

"Hey, you." He smiled down at her and gave her a kiss on her forehead. Then he walked around the table to hug Breena and kiss her cheek. "I was looking for you earlier. Happy to find you here," he said softly, sitting next to her.

She grinned at him. "We hardly get to see each other. I arranged with Grace to stay with Kelly so I could come here tonight."

"Excellent plan." He looked across to Gina and Carly. "So what have you ladies been up to today?"

He sat and listened while Carly shared every detail of her day. Gabriel looked around at these women and realized this was his family. Of course Carly was, but Breena and Gina were too. And he liked the idea of having a bigger family.

After Carly was done sharing, he followed Breena into the kitchen and wrapped her in a hug. "Thanks for being here. I like coming home to this. To you." He rested his head on top of hers and felt his heart settle into place.

"So..." She looked up at him a little hesitantly. "What time are the buses leaving tomorrow?"

"Around eight o'clock in the morning. They're going to drive all day and night to get to Los Angeles in time to set up for the show."

"I'll come by and see Carly tomorrow. If that's okay."

"Sure, anytime. She loves having you visit. *I* love having you visit." He leaned down to kiss her. "Now, please tell me what smells so good. I mean, besides you." He leaned in and sniffed her dramatically, making her laugh.

He couldn't quite put his finger on it, but something felt off tonight. Like Breena was holding back.

Chapter 29

BREENA

THE NEXT MORNING, THE apartment felt empty with both Laci and Kelly gone. They'd left before she could make breakfast, but at least she was able to say goodbye and give them each a big hug. She and Grace had a quiet breakfast together before Grace headed out to see what progress Carl was making on the mountain cabin she was turning into a shelter for abused women and children. It sounded like Hope's House would be operational by the summer.

After Grace left, Breena spent some time baking cookies. It was Valentine's Day, so she decided to take some heart-shaped cookies to Gina and Carly for them to decorate.

After the cookies cooled, she packaged them up and headed to Gabe's. She was going to miss him terribly for the next three weeks. Last night, she couldn't bring herself to talk about it, but she knew his job was his priority.

Pulling up behind his house, she was surprised to see his car still there. He must have taken a taxi that morning to get to the bus. She grabbed the container with the cookies, headed to the back door, and waited for Gina to answer her knock.

"Well, good morning, beautiful." Gabe was standing in the doorway, wearing jeans, a blue-and-black flannel shirt, and socks.

"But..." She couldn't form the words. She was so stunned to see him. "What are you doing here?"

"Well, I live here." He laughed. "Where am I supposed to be?"

"On tour."

He looked at her, his brow knitting together. "I'm not going on the tour. I thought you knew that."

She could feel her eyes welling up, though she wasn't sure why she felt like crying.

"No. Kelly is going, and we have a tour manager. Between them, they can handle anything that comes up."

"But..." she paused. "I thought you always went on tour with Laci."

"I used to, yes. But my priorities have changed, and it didn't make sense to go this time. Besides, I didn't *want* to go."

She tried to process this information. "I guess I always thought work was your top priority."

He frowned a little at the comment. "No, family has always been my top priority. I worked so hard for so long because I needed to be able to take care of Carly. When I saw how they weren't taking care of her at Happy Valley, I knew I needed to make a change. I guess I was ready for the change because it has all fallen into place relatively easily."

"I'm glad Carly is your priority. She seems to be settling in well with you. I know she loves seeing you every day. She mentioned it yesterday."

He smiled, "I'm glad to have her here. It's good for both of us.".

He must have realized she still wasn't getting what he was trying to tell her. "What I said was my *family* is my priority. Yes, Carly is my family. But so are you, Bree. At least, I think of you that way. You are part of the reason I'm not going on the tour."

Her eyes widened. "I...oh."

"For so many years, I pushed everyone except Carly and Laci away. And for all those years, they were my only family. Since you've been in my life, my family has expanded exponentially. Carl and Grace and Jillian are part of my circle now. The Marshalls. Oh, and I just brought in a business partner, Jackson. You'll meet him soon, I'm sure. So...yeah. Family. Besides, how could I leave you?" He brushed a tear off her cheek.

He hadn't left her. For the first time in a long time, she was someone's priority. He pulled her in for a hug, and she wrapped her arms around his waist, breathing in the scent that would forever remind her of Gabe.

She closed her eyes so she could remember this moment.

Epilogue

BREENA

HAND IN HAND, BREENA and Gabe walked across the street in front of Gabe's townhouse and down the half block to Amati's. Spring was finally showing itself, and the middle of March was proving to be a beautiful time to be in Nashville. The trees were starting to leaf, tulips were blooming all around the city, and the weather was finally warm enough to not lug around a big jacket.

Parked in front of the restaurant were the tour buses, unloading the band, the crew, the singers, everyone who was part of the tour. All pouring into Amati's for a night of celebration. The first leg of the tour was over, and it had been a success.

Walking in, they were greeted with a cacophony of noise and delicious scents. Within seconds, they each received a glass of wine and a hug from Mrs. Amati. As they made their way through the rowdy crowd, Gabe spoke to every single person. Usually by name. And if he didn't know a name, he made sure to ask. They made their way to Laci, Jillian, and Grace, who were talking off to one side.

Gabe leaned down closer to Breena. "I'll be back in a few minutes." He kissed her on the side of her head, and she watched him work his way through the crowd to a small microphone and speaker he'd set up earlier in the day. He stood on one of the chairs and tapped the mic.

"Can you all hear me?" His voice boomed from the speaker. Hands flew to cover ears as Gabe fiddled with some dials and tried again. "Sorry about that. How does this sound? Welcome home to everyone who was part of the tour. This is our first time hosting a post-tour dinner, so thank you all for coming and for bringing your families."

Breena looked around in amazement at all the people it took to put on a tour. From the sounds of it, the learning curve hadn't been horrible and it went well.

"In case you didn't know, the tour so far is a smashing success." He raised his wine glass. "So thank you one and all. Here's to our tour family."

There were lots of cheers and clinking of glasses. Breena touched glasses with her friends as well as a few of the crew she hadn't yet met.

"The Amatis have prepared an amazing feast for all of us tonight. Everyone, find a seat, please. They will serve everything family style, meaning each dish is to serve your whole table. So take some of whatever is in front of you, then pass it around. Be patient with the waitstaff who are working hard for us tonight. Enjoy, ladies and gentlemen."

Breena watched him step down from the chair and work his way back to her. He sidled up next to her. "Can I steal you for a minute? There's someone I think you want to meet."

"Sure." Her curiosity was up. "Who am I meeting?"

"You'll see." He grabbed her hand, and they worked their way to one of the back corners of the room. On the way through, Gabe continued to greet everyone as they made their way through the tables.

At the back of the restaurant, in the direction they were headed, Breena saw Mr. Amati talking with another man. She could only see him from the back and didn't recognize him as someone she'd met before. He had reddish hair that looked like it was starting to gray at the temples. He was dressed in khakis and a white button-down shirt, long sleeves rolled up to the elbows. Gabe led her up to the men, and when he turned around, Breena's mouth fell open.

"How... you're here." For so long, Breena hadn't wanted to meet her father. But after the last few months of communicating with him, she'd started dreaming of it.

And now, somehow, he was here. She looked back and forth between her father and Gabe.

Gabe spoke first. "I hope you don't mind me taking the liberty of inviting Peter to the party tonight."

She smiled at Gabe, then turned to her father and hugged him. His arms went around her, and it felt just like she'd always thought a hug from a dad would feel. She closed her eyes and just took in the moment.

As they broke apart, she smiled at him. "It's a pleasure to finally meet you. In person." She turned to Gabe. "Thank you."

He put an arm around her shoulders. "Tonight is all about family, so I thought you might want yours here." He shook Peter's hand. "I'm glad you could make it. Thanks for coming all this way."

"It was an offer I couldn't refuse." Looking at Breena, Peter continued. "After Cindy died, I didn't think I'd ever have family again. It is such a gift to have you in my life now."

When bellies were full and hunger sated, the staff cleared the dinner plates and got ready to serve dessert and coffee. Breena was seated at a table with Gabe, her father, Grace and Carl, Jillian, Kelly, and Laci. Peter was planning to stay a few days, and she was looking forward to spending more time with him.

Gabe had his arm around her shoulders across the back of her chair, but he seemed distracted and kept looking around. His hand was tapping the chair behind her back and his leg was bouncing up and down.

Breena leaned over. "You okay?"

He looked a little startled. "Oh, yeah. I'm good." He stopped tapping the back of her chair and his leg was now still, but his eyes kept roaming the room.

As soon as the tables were cleared, Laci excused herself and walked up to the microphone. "Since y'all are sitting down, I'm not going to stand on a chair like Gabe did." She chuckled. "I just wanted to add my two cents and say thank you to everyone here. Because of you—all of you—I looked good out there these past few weeks. We had a few new folks join the family, and from what I saw, you all fit in seamlessly."

She held her glass up to honor the group as a whole before continuing. "I'd like to personally thank Kelly for making my life so much easier these last few weeks. You kept me on track, on time, and in the right city."

Laci laughed, making Breena wonder if there was a story there. Breena glanced over at Kelly and saw her cheeks were bright red.

"Anyway, it's good to be home. Now I happen to know the Amatis make an incredible dessert, so let's enjoy whatever delights they have created for us tonight." She turned the microphone off and worked her way back to the table, stopping to talk to many along the way.

Breena settled back in her chair not, sure how she was going to fit dessert in; she was already so full. She watched as the waitstaff descended on the tables to serve a beautiful tiramisu to everyone.

The waiter served Gabe, then stepped around to Breena's other side. "No, thank you." She waved him off. "I'm stuffed."

She saw him look at Gabe then back. "Maybe you can share it with someone, ma'am."

She smiled at him. "No but thank you. It looks delicious."

Again, she saw him look at Gabe, as if waiting for further instructions. It was starting to frustrate her. She turned to Gabe.

"I don't want any dessert. I'm stuffed. Why would he need to get your approval to not give me a piece of tiramisu?" she whispered through clenched teeth.

"I...ah...hmm. Yes, well that would be my fault, I'm afraid." At her look, Gabe picked up her hand and kissed her palm. He took a deep breath. "Breena darling, I would never presume you couldn't make your own decisions about anything. You are the most capable woman I know. But I asked for something a little different on your plate, which is why poor Thomas is looking to me for advice."

Confused, she turned back to the waiter, only to see he'd already set a dessert plate in front of her. Instead of a lovely piece of tiramisu, there was a red rose, a lavender rose, another light pink flower she couldn't identify, and a small black velvet box.

She could feel her eyes go wide and her heartbeat double. She looked back at Gabe. Questioning.

He reached over and picked up the lavender flower. "This one"—he handed it to her—"represents love at first sight. You took my breath away the first time I saw you, and you continue to do so."

Breena blinked back the threatening tears and took a deep breath.

Gabe picked up the red rose. "And this one represents love. I love you and will always love you." He handed her the rose, then picked up the third flower. "Do you know what this one is?"

She shook her head.

"Well, I'm not going to tell you to look it up." He grinned at her. "This is a peony, and a peony represents a happy marriage."

He picked up the black box from her plate, then scooched his chair back a bit from the table. In one smooth move, he was on one knee in front of her. He held up the little box that held her full attention, and he opened it.

"When I saw this, I immediately knew I was meant to give it to you."

She looked down at the ring in the box. She was stunned to see a spectacular flower-shaped diamond ring. It was perfect—a round center diamond surrounded by ten small teardrop diamonds, fanning out like petals.

She looked into Gabe's eyes and saw tenderness and love, along with the nerves she'd noted earlier in the evening. "Breena, I love you more than I thought it was possible to love another person. Will you do me the honor of marrying me?"

Breena looked at him. She could see sweat forming on his upper lip as he waited for her answer. "I remember hearing one time that when making a decision, if it's not a hell yes, then it's a no. This, Gabriel van Neugh, is definitely a hell yes! I will most definitely marry you. Now put that gorgeous ring on my finger."

She saw the relief on his face as he pulled her in for a kiss. Thunder sounded around them as the whole restaurant exploded in applause. She'd forgotten they were surrounded by people.

Gabe leaned back just enough to put the ring on the third finger of her left hand, then held it up for all to see.

Joyfully, he shouted, "She said yes!"

Ready for what's next? Jillian Montgomery gets her story told in *Discovering Jillian*

You can download the book here: https://www. amazon.com/dp/1960969080/

If you enjoyed this book, please take a few minutes to **leave a review**. https://www.amazon.com/dp/B0C 5BCVWFK

Authors really appreciate this, it helps Amazon know my book is worth sharing with other readers, and it helps other readers know this is a book they might like.

Thank you!

About the author

Becki Lee is a sweet contemporary romance author that loves to throw in a dash of humor, good friends, and good looking heroes. You can read more about future books on **her website.** (https://beckileeauth or.com/)

Acknowledgements

I have been extraordinarily blessed with an amazing community around me.

My family has been so supportive. This endeavor has affected our time, travel and finances, and I am grateful to have the space, support and love to pursue this passion.

To my sprint partners - Leah, Ann, Marian, Christine, Kate, Kerry, and everyone else who has helped keep me on track with my writing. Writing sprints have magical powers on helping me get words on the page.

I am most appreciative of my beta readers - Samantha and Christy for your words of wisdom when mine didn't make any sense.

Thank you to Rachel for your long hours of taking out all the extra words and commas. I do love commas.

Thank you to all the readers who have enjoyed Finding Dolly and have reached out with kind words. I hope you enjoy Breena's story as well.

And I'm very grateful to God for an overactive imagination and an overabundance of crazy story ideas. I pray and endeavor to do your words and ideas justice.

Also by Becki Lee

Nashville Hearts series

Rescuing Hope (prequel)
Finding Dolly
Dating Breena
Discovering Jillian
Marrying Grace

Nashville Billionaire series

Betting on Brian
Remembering Beau
Always Alex: a Christmas Novella (coming Christmas
2024)

Hang out with Becki:

Facebook https://www.facebook.com/beckilee author

Goodreads https://www.goodreads.com/author/show/29882237.Becki_Lee

Amazon https://www.amazon.com/author/beckileeauthor

Instagram https://www.instagram.com/beckile_author/